Anthony

The Survivor Series, Volume 4

JP Barnaby

Published by Recovery Romance Press, 2024.

This is a work of fiction. Similarities to real people, places, or events are entirely coincidental.

ANTHONY

First edition. November 11, 2024.

Copyright © 2024 JP Barnaby.

ISBN: 979-8230381891

Written by JP Barnaby.

Also by JP Barnaby

The Survivor Series
Aaron
Ben
Spencer
Anthony

Watch for more at www.jpbarnabyauthor.com.

Table of Contents

Chapter One 1
Chapter Two 21
Chapter Three 35
Chapter Four 39
Chapter Five 57
Chapter Six 75
Chapter Seven 83
Chapter Eight 101
Chapter Nine 107
Chapter Ten 111
Chapter Eleven 123
Chapter Twelve 133
Chapter Thirteen 141
Chapter Fourteen 145
Chapter Fifteen 149
Chapter Sixteen 159
Chapter Seventeen 165
Chapter Eighteen 175
Chapter Nineteen 183
Chapter Twenty 193
Chapter Twenty-One 201
Chapter Twenty-Two 209
Chapter Twenty-Three 223

For Aaron Downing, whose voice I hear in my head every day. I promised you a happy ending for your brother, baby. I hope it helps to clear the burdens on your heart.

For Jodi, without whom this book would have been completely wrong. Thank you for asking the perfect question.

And finally, for my Cody. I promised you a cover the day I met you. I was just waiting for the book that would do you justice. You are a beautiful, kind, and loving soul. Yes, sometimes you're a mess, but you're my mess and I wouldn't have it any other way. I love you, kiddo.

Chapter One

Anthony Downing slammed the basement window open, daring them to catch him. He'd finished high school; they couldn't say shit to him anymore. When no one came down the stairs, barking for him to go back to bed, he stood on his mattress and lobbed an unopened bottle of Absolut up to the unkempt grass outside—grass he should have cut that morning; grass he didn't give a fuck about. He hoisted himself up, ripping his jeans on a jagged piece of the metal windowsill. It missed his skin by a breath, and he wished it hadn't, wished for the pain so he could feel something other than numbness.

Smothered by his parents' indifference, a soul-deep need for freedom drove him into the cool night air.

A faint chill clung to his skin, and he caught the soft scent of burning as he bent to pick up his vodka. Someone must have been using a fire pit in the quiet of a Saturday night in suburbia. Anthony liked the smell. It reminded him of the backyard barbecues they'd thrown when his family was whole. Before Aaron proved Copernicus wrong and became the center of the fucking universe.

Before Anthony became the invisible boy.

He scanned the side of the house and the yard beyond, searching for any witness to his flight, but saw no one. Neither of his parents seemed to notice that their seventeen-year-old son had crawled out the window for yet another night of debauchery. They'd rather watch the news, celebrating their newfound freedom from Aaron's madness.

Just once, Anthony wished they'd ask him to join them. He'd fucking watch the paint peel if it meant getting out of the basement and back into their lives. He'd even contend with their constant disappointment. Anything, if they'd just notice he was still there.

Headlights moved past his house, and Anthony glanced up with grim determination. After one final check of the dark windows over his shoulder, he ghosted across the lawn toward the street. The beat-to-fuck Dodge stopped a few houses down, and Anthony headed that way. At some point, the car had been blue, but the primer seemed to have spread since then. Chase loved to work on the thing, only he never actually finished any of the projects he started. He replaced the bumper but never painted it. Hot rims took priority over balding tires. The rumbling engine idled when Chase pulled up to the curb, and Anthony grabbed the door handle with another glance back at the darkened street. He climbed in the passenger seat and whipped the door closed behind him.

"Hey." Chase barely waited for Anthony to hold up the bottle of booze, his ticket to ride, before gunning down the rest of the street.

"Hey."

"Nice nails, Princess."

"Fuck off." Chase's dig stung. So what if he'd gotten bored in math and colored them in with a black Sharpie. Everybody did it. It was the princess bit that got to him. All of Chase's recent throwaway comments about his sexuality pissed him off. Anthony liked guys. It wasn't a secret. He didn't hide how he felt about Chase, either. Why the fucking shade now? They'd been friends for years.

He glanced at his friend around the edges of his hoodie. Chase's greasy, blond hair hung in lank curtains on either side of a pale face. His shadowed eyes and unshaven jaw betrayed every late night party they'd hit that week. The rumpled button-up worn over clean jeans showed at least some effort to be respectable, an effort Anthony hadn't shared. He hadn't wandered by a mirror lately, but given his mother's increased bitching, Anthony figured he must look pretty rough. His hair, grown out to a dull brown, hung in his face no matter what he did with it. At least it covered his painfully average looks. He'd have killed for his father's crystal-blue eyes, but Aaron got those, just like he got everything else. Anthony had ended up with the leftover dull brown instead. His clear, pale skin probably glowed in the dark with how little it saw the sun. And even as tall and lanky as he was, somehow he'd also gotten feet too big for his body.

It all came together in a package custom-made for the back of a discount shelf.

So yeah, he fucking colored his nails black with a Sharpie.

"Dude, when are you gonna grow some balls and start driving yourself to this shit?" Chase flipped a cigarette butt into the quaint suburban night. Not another soul occupied the street right then. The two of them were alone, a bright future of hard edges against the two-car garages and white picket fences.

"You know the Mustang sounds like a plane landing when I start it up. You want the night to end before it ever starts?" Anthony couldn't hide the petulance in his voice. He hated it, but goddamn, couldn't he find just one person who didn't look at him like a fucking burden?

"You're practically eighteen, Downer, a fucking adult. Why do you give a shit what they say?"

"I've got a month. And that's easy for you to say. Your parents don't give a fuck about anything you do. They just throw money at you to make you go away."

"I'm not sure which is worse."

After a minute of silence, Anthony spoke again. "They're on me again about college."

"Yeah, mine are too."

"My mom rubbed it in my face that even *Aaron* went to college. Because everything in the fucking universe revolves around *Aaron*."

"Did they give you the 'if you want to live under our roof' shit?"

"Yep. It's their way or the highway."

"Wouldn't they flip their shit if we chose the highway?"

Chase turned up the volume on his car radio and fiddled with the iPod plugged into the aux port. Anthony watched in disbelief. Chase couldn't mean they'd just leave, could he?

With one hand on the wheel and one eye on the road, Chase flipped through his seemingly infinite playlist and switched to a song Anthony had never heard. He didn't comment because Chase wouldn't be able to hear him over the music anyway. Instead, Anthony leaned back in the seat and stared out the window, picking at the bits of marker on the skin where he'd missed the nail. For a long time, he wondered if maybe they could leave. If they could have a different life. Maybe they could even have one together.

Too bad he was too much of a fucking coward to ask.

The song hadn't ended by the time Chase rolled to a stop in front of a ramshackle house on the wrong side of town from where they'd grown up. Anthony hadn't been there before, but since the place belonged to Skylar Logan and his junkie mother, Anthony figured it would be one hell of a party. They pulled up behind a soft-top Jeep and climbed out of the car. Anthony reached back in and grabbed the vodka. The edge of his favorite Outbreak Monkey T-shirt caught on the broken piece of window handle, and he pulled it away gently. There were few things he gave a shit about. That shirt topped the small list.

"Dude, I can't believe Jenny left her Jeep open like that around here. Dumbass. We should fuck with it just because we can."

Chase stopped on the sidewalk in front of the red Jeep and peered inside. Anthony put a hand on his arm when he made to open his fly. His words caught on the dryness in his mouth.

ANTHONY

"Come on, I want a drink, and Jenny's okay." He didn't want Chase messing with Jenny. An assload of people at school gave him shit on daily basis, because of his music, his looks, or his freak brother, but Jenny didn't. Her older sister Kerri had dated Allen for a while. Plenty of those fuckheads deserved to have their cars messed with, but not her.

Anthony dragged Chase by a belt loop and jerked the screen door open, rattling it on busted hinges. The erratic bass thumped in his shoes as they crossed the threshold into the house. A beer can lay on its side in the entryway. Wasted amber liquid pooled around the half-crushed aluminum. They stepped over it and a girl sprawled on the floor. Leaning against the wall, she stared at them with a glazed look in her dilated eyes. Battered tile gave way to stained carpeting when they came out of the short hall and into a family room filled with people from school lounging in various states of drunken mess.

Trisha Marik straddled the big junior Gavin Carter on one of the low couches. Their high school football coach would kill Gavin if he saw where his star player was right then. Gavin held up a capsule for little Trisha to take. She smiled at him and opened her mouth. He slid the pill between her lips, and she sucked his thumb with an erotic twist of her tongue.

Stupid trusting fucks.

Chase's brother had taught them at the very first party he'd ever taken them to: never take something unless you knew what it was. Never take shit someone else gave you, and for fuck's sake, never leave your cup of booze unattended. Don't follow those rules and, guy or girl, you'll end up the ass-up, head-down cum dumpster of the football team.

Anthony weaved around a drunken couple dancing with their hands in places he didn't need to see and followed Chase into the kitchen. Skylar stood next to the sink with his tongue down the throat of some girl Anthony didn't recognize. Their host must have picked her up on the side of the road somewhere with the promise of drugs and booze.

"Hey, where do you want this shit?" Chase held up the bottle of Absolut and two baggies of unidentified pills.

"Nice," the girl said as they finally came up for air.

Skylar grinned. "Throw it on the counter over there with the cups Gina brought. Isn't she pretty?" He slid a crooked finger under her chin. She giggled and Anthony wanted to vomit. Instead, he cracked open the Absolut, grabbed a cup, and poured himself a drink. At least if he drank from his own bottle, he knew it was good quality and no one had messed with it. The others just took what they could get.

Stupid. Trusting. Fucks.

"Come on." Chase washed down two pills, ones he'd brought, with a drink from Anthony's cup. Anthony watched the muscles in his throat work and tried not to get hard. Fuck, that's all he'd need, these jocks seeing him pop wood over his best friend. Half the school already thought they were fucking. Anthony wouldn't have cared if he were actually getting sex out of it. Since it was just a rumor, it only depressed him. Just like at home, the only time anyone at school saw him, they were giving him shit.

Being invisible was exhausting. Like bouncing off transparent walls in an attempt to escape, only no one else sees the walls.

Ever.

ANTHONY

Anthony tagged behind Chase as they did the obligatory tour of the house, which always served to make them feel either better or worse about their lives, depending on what they found. Skylar's house made Anthony feel way better about his life. The place was a dump, a tiny two-bedroom house with one floor, tube televisions, and no imagination.

Chase continued through the only hall, marked by four closed doors. He tried the first door on the left, but the lock didn't give. As they started to move away, a gruff voice yelled from the other side that he'd be out in a minute. They'd found the bathroom. Good to know. Anthony tried the door on the right and found it unlocked. As he pushed it open, a high-pitched squeak made him jump. Two girls pulled a blanket over their naked skin just a second too late, and his face flushed with heat.

"Sorry," he mumbled, closing the door before he got a real education in female anatomy. Chase would probably have gone in and tried to join them, but Anthony had never had the desire. Well, unless Chase wanted to....

Two more doors and they could return as champions, the Lewis and Clark of high school parties. Again, Chase took the one on the left and found a linen closet full of towels, spare toilet paper, and a teenage couple making out so hard they didn't even notice the door open. The guy Anthony couldn't place, since the girl seemed to be swallowing his face, but there was no mistaking Sarah Mitchell's purple-streaked blond hair. Her shirt shifted higher as the guy's hand fondled her under it. Chase snorted before closing the door. Sarah Mitchell had been a party legend since Anthony and Chase were freshmen. He had no idea how she wasn't pregnant or dead.

Anthony turned the knob for the last door, the room on the right, and its emptiness surprised him. He stepped in followed closely by Chase. The hairs on the back of his neck stood up as Chase shifted behind him, awareness prickling through his skin. A light flared on overhead, and Anthony turned to see Chase looking around.

They never stole anything at these parties. Most of the houses where they partied had nothing to steal anyway, and this one didn't disappoint. A worn quilt lay strewn across the lumpy bed, threadbare and from some generation other than theirs. Someone had pushed the bed against the far wall, but a folding tray table hugged its side. It was slick with dust and a film of something foul beneath the round yellowing lace thing that decorated it. A ticking alarm clock broke the monotony of thumping bass from the party in full swing down the hall.

Anthony walked past the framed pictures, DVDs, and random spare change thrown carelessly on the dresser. A collection of spoons with names of states hung on this wall, and the cloying scent of incense did nothing to mask the smell of cigarette smoke mixed with pot. Mismatched junk preserved in a cheap shadow box hung on a bit of wall covered in ancient, floral wallpaper. It looked like something his mother would have. Before the world changed, he remembered her collecting little angels. After Aaron came home, she must have lost her faith in them. One more thing Aaron had taken from his family.

"I feel good. Let's just stay in here for a while." Chase dropped down to sit on the side of the bed, and Anthony swallowed hard. His dick rubbed against his fly. Yes, he wanted to stay in the bedroom with Chase. He wanted to do a lot of things with Chase. They'd shared a couple of clumsy hand jobs in Anthony's room when they were drunk, but it surprised him when Chase opened his fly. He had his cock in his hand before Anthony could blink.

"Come here," Chase said, and Anthony's dick almost exploded in his pants. *God, yeah.*

ANTHONY

The room seemed so much bigger when he crossed it to stand in front of Chase. They looked at each other for a long moment, Chase with his dick in his hand, Anthony's stretching the denim on the front of his jeans.

Anthony glanced around the bare room again, trying to find his sanity. He never thought they'd be doing this in a million years. He turned, took two steps in the claustrophobic room, and locked the door. No reason to tempt fate, even if they were graduating in a couple days.

"You got a purdy mouth," Chase drawled with a wicked grin.

"Shut up." Anthony turned to face him. "If you want something, fucking ask for it."

"Suck me off?" Chase asked with quiet, halting words. They were about to cross a big fucking line in the sand, and they both knew it.

Chase's legs scorched the outside of Anthony's thighs as he stood between them. A decision hung heavy and harsh in the air. God, he wanted it. He'd jacked off thinking about it for four years. Anthony stared down at Chase, his face flushed and his eyes wild from the pills. The way his jeans cut across the tops of his thighs made Anthony's mouth water. He'd done it before, trading blowjobs for pills when he'd been jonesing, but that was before his parents stuck him in rehab. Besides, this was so fucking different.

"Fine." Anthony used a palm on each of Chase's legs for balance when he lowered himself to the floor between Chase's feet.

Chase rested back on his hands as Anthony wrapped his own around Chase's dick and began with light strokes. A moan started deep in the back of Chase's throat but barely escaped his pursed lips. Anthony leaned in and swiped his tongue across the head of Chase's dick, eliciting a sharp gasp. He drew the head in, sucking as the swollen mushroom passed his lips. Chase's moan told Anthony all he needed to know. He had Chase right where he wanted him.

Well, until he opened his fucking mouth.

"Fuck that's good. I knew you were a fag," Chase murmured.

Anthony stopped for just a moment, letting the words puncture a hole in him wide enough for the shock to seep through. He should have seen it coming. Throughout their friendship, they could only trade hand jobs in the dark of night, and Chase would always sleep on the floor when he stayed over, never in bed with Anthony. So many little things to tell Anthony he disgusted Chase. He'd always clung to the delusion that one day they could be more, but it broke into a thousand jagged pieces with Chase's words.

Still, he couldn't stop himself from sucking harder, desperate to erase the words from his mind, to impress Chase. He didn't want Chase to feel only disgust when they touched. Anthony wrapped a hand around Chase's cock, stroking the bit that didn't fit in his mouth. He'd done this probably a dozen times before, but it had never meant as much to him as it did then. They were on the razor's edge—one wrong step and he could lose the best friend he'd ever had. Some days, Chase seemed like the *only* friend Anthony had ever had.

Anthony pressed his forearms to the bed on either side of Chase's hips. It was the closest they'd ever been to an embrace. Chase's deep groan drowned out the sucking sounds Anthony's mouth made around the dick driving into it. He moved his head, massaging Chase's length with his lips, increasing the suction, trying anything he could to blow Chase's mind.

Instead, he just got Chase's load.

"Fuck...." Chase moaned as he shot into Anthony's mouth. Color blossomed high on his cheeks as his eyes slammed closed. Anthony watched through long bangs and hooded eyelids, swallowing against the bitter taste of pain as Chase jerked forward, pushing Anthony off his prick. Anthony stretched up and realized an instant too late Chase had turned his head away from kiss he wanted so fucking badly.

ANTHONY

"Dude, I'm not fucking like you," Chase spat, pulling his jeans up as he stood. "Get up off the floor, man." Chase waited just long enough for Anthony to regain his feet before he exploded out of the bedroom.

Tears stung Anthony's eyes, and a burn that had nothing to do with Chase's cock wound its way up his throat. God, he fucking hated Chase some days.

The bathroom door was open when he walked out of the bedroom and back up the hall. Without waiting to see where Chase went, he ducked into the small room, tugging the door closed behind him, and popped open the medicine cabinet. He thanked God for the lack of drugs, because right then, he might have been tempted.

Fuck rehab.

Instead, he grabbed the toothpaste. His finger worked as a makeshift toothbrush, if for no other reason than to get the come off his tongue. He wished he could wipe the remnants of Chase's hate from his mind as easily.

He dropped the toilet lid and sat down. In all the years they'd been friends, Chase had never bothered enough to get to know him. No one could miss Anthony's sexuality—he didn't hide it—and he certainly took enough shit at school for it. How could Chase not have known? Did he really pay so little attention to Anthony? Did he not care at all?

Anthony remained sitting in the bathroom, his head in his hands, for what seemed like hours. A hammering on the door told him he'd been in there for a while, though, so he flushed the empty toilet and washed his hands as he gathered himself. Finally, when Anthony could stall no longer, he opened the door to a red-faced girl and stepped aside just in time for her to puke all over the closed toilet lid. He left her to it and went to refill his drink.

A crowd had gathered in the living room, and Anthony stepped around it, uninterested in whoever was under the beer bong or who had a mouth on someone else's body part. Instead, he bypassed the gawkers and wandered into the kitchen. Only Skylar's wraparound chick stood among the mostly empty bottles. Anthony grabbed the Absolut he'd brought and tipped it to his lips without stopping to wonder whether some sick fuck had added anything else to the mix. All three swallows went down easy, and he embraced the burn around Chase's semen.

"Hey." The girl turned her bleary gaze toward him. "Have you seen Chase?"

She cocked her head as if she'd be able to hear him better at an angle. The vodka scorched his nearly empty stomach. Remnants of the frozen pizza he'd had for dinner hours before were clearly no match for the booze, and his image of her blurred a little around the edges.

"You mean that guy you came in with? The one with the hair?"

"Yeah."

"Dude, he's right there."

Anthony followed the direction of her raised hand as it pointed the way to his own heartbreak. There, in the middle of the living room, Chase sat on the low, stained couch with Jenny bouncing on his dick as the rest of the party cheered them on. In their position, Anthony could only see her back, but the fiery red hair gave her away. The intensity in Chase's face, visible from the side vantage point, made the vodka rebel against his insides. Clearly, he enjoyed her sexual attention. Nothing like the discomfort he'd had with Anthony in the bedroom a little while before.

Anthony wondered with detached interest what he'd taken to get it up again so fast.

ANTHONY

"Pfft... I love pussy. Downer doesn't know what he's missing." Chase's gaze fell on Anthony, who wondered if Chase could see the wind knocked out of his lungs by the bold statement delivered in front of the crowd. The vodka burned his esophagus as it tried to come back up, but Anthony ignored it. He looked away, not wanting to encourage Chase to make any more hurtful remarks. As much as he'd love to tell Chase to fuck off and walk home, they were too far away. He had to watch and wait for Chase to have his fun before they could think about leaving.

For a split second, he thought about calling someone to get him. Fucking Allen and his fucking Purdue fucking education would have been his first choice, but he could walk home faster than Allen could get there. Aaron had moved off with Spencer a few months back, so they were too far away too. His parents would flip their shit and send his ass back to rehab.

He had no one. No one at all.

Instead of listening to Chase's grunts and Jenny's high-pitched cries, Anthony turned and walked into the backyard, closing the door behind him. The glass door deadened the sound of chaos and partying on the other side. While he could make out rhythmic chanting, he couldn't decipher the words. He would have to wait for Chase to tire himself out, to prove his heterosexuality, with any girl at the party who would spread for him.

The predawn air worked its way through his clothes, chilling every part of him. He couldn't decide if the freeze came from the cold or his own heart when he replayed Chase's words again and again in his head.

Hate would keep him warm.

In the moonlight pooled near his feet, a plastic birdbath lay on its side. Anthony wondered if Skylar or his mother thought the birdbath gave them a bit of respectability or if it had simply been on sale during one of their drugged-out afternoons. Movement caught his attention, and he watched a possum as it scurried between patches of tall grass. Anthony froze as it stopped and turned in his direction, its glassy eyes glowing in the reflected porch light.

"Hey, little guy," Anthony whispered, not wanting to break the tenuous peace between them. He'd felt so alone sitting under the stars, waiting for the end of a lifelong friendship. The possum skittered to the right about a foot and stopped again. Anthony felt ridiculously desperate to keep his companion out there in the dark.

He held a quiet, one-sided conversation with the possum while he waited.

It took a long time for Chase to fuck himself straight again.

After he'd spent about an hour talking to a wild animal and tracing the lines and imperfections in the plastic birdbath, the door opened behind him.

"Come on, loser, let's go shopping." Chase's voice cut through the stillness with sharp precision. Anthony took one last look around the yard, but his furry companion had skittered off in fear. He understood that, so he pulled himself to his feet.

Heat scorched his face when Chase led him back through the kitchen. People stopped midsentence to stare and start whispered conversations as he passed. It shouldn't unnerve him, but it did. He had to live there. He had to start college with some of them in the fall. Worse, he had to walk past them to get to that diploma in a few days. God, what kind of insults would they scream for everyone to hear?

ANTHONY

Silence sliced through the tattered remains of their friendship on the drive back to Anthony's house. They didn't talk about the enormous Indian elephant stuffed in Chase's backseat, its trunk hanging out the window in the dark. One street turned into the next, and Anthony couldn't find his balls long enough to confront Chase about the venom and hatred he'd spewed. In truth, he didn't want to hear more. Instead, he stared out the window, watching the familiar landmarks of his youth roll past in the muted light of the periodic street lamps.

When they reached his street, Anthony didn't hesitate. Even before the car came to a complete stop two houses away from his own, he flung the car door open. The short screech of overused brakes preceded the slam of his car door only by seconds. Anthony didn't even turn when Chase sped off, leaving him alone on the side of the road.

Beyond caring about recklessness, Anthony didn't try to quiet his reentry to the house as he fell through the window onto his bed. No sound came from the upper floors. No one even knew he'd gone. Most of the time, no one knew he was *there*, either.

His clothes landed on the floor in angry disarray. Sleep shorts forgotten, he more fell into bed than climbed. The weight of the evening pushed him onto the mattress.

The more he tried to close his eyes and sleep, the more oblivion eluded him. Defeated, Anthony grabbed a gaming controller from his side table and powered on the Xbox at the foot of his bed. Mindless building of a vast cubical world generally relaxed him enough for sleep. As a bonus, his friends, the ones who really understood him, resided in that world. He'd found them through online parties and cherished the nameless, faceless people all over the country who didn't judge him or ignore him.

Sometimes, they were more real to him than the flesh-and-blood people in his life.

Within five minutes of logging into a game, he had a chat message from Jay. If he still believed in the concept of best friends after tonight, Jay would have come in a close second to Chase. They talked every night after Anthony got home from school. The conversations ranged from school to gaming to boyfriends and recently turned into something else. Jay started coming on to him, sending him pictures that made his cock stand at attention. He loved the shy way Jay looked at the camera when he took naked selfies for Anthony. Jay probably saw the same shyness in the pictures he sent back. He'd never sexted anyone before, but it made him feel wanted for the first time in his life.

[Jay]: Hey babe, I missed you. Good party?

Anthony smiled, warmth returning to his fingertips for the first time in hours. He grabbed the micro keyboard and popped it into place on the bottom of the controller. Jay didn't have a Kinect like everyone else on the planet, so they couldn't video or audio chat. He only existed as words on a screen, but he was more real to Anthony than any other friend he'd ever had.

Well, except Chase. Fucking Chase.

[Anthony]: It sucked.

Understatement of the year, Downer.

[Jay]: What happened?

Shame welled in the pit of Anthony's stomach as he thought about it.

[Anthony]: I blew Chase at the party and he called me a fag.

[Jay]: What a douche. You deserve better than that.

His heart lifted, and he sat up a little higher on the bed. Another message indicator popped on the screen, and he opened it.

[Jay]: If you were with me, I'd never hurt you.

God, if only that were true. It didn't really matter though, because Jay lived in Detroit. He might as well have been on the moon. They couldn't date in any real way, but after Chase and the party, he wanted to be wanted.

Jay's face flashed in his mind, and he grabbed the laptop from his bedroom floor between the bed and dresser. It took a minute to power up, during which Jay stayed silent on the screen. Anthony entered his password, clicked around into the folder structure, and opened his special folder titled *System Files*. He'd chosen the name because it was something his mother would overlook if she ever got into his laptop. In a subfolder marked *Jay*, he double-clicked his very favorite picture, and Jay appeared on the screen.

He said they'd been at a family event, and he stood arm in arm with someone the camera didn't catch, maybe his dad. They stood behind their house in a summer explosion of green. Anthony loved the soft, shy look on Jay's face. He wasn't smiling, but his expression could have broken into a smile given a chance. Long lashes rimmed his dark eyes, and short brown hair ended in subtle curls around his face. A smattering of freckles dusted his upper cheeks and nose, making him look younger than seventeen.

[Jay]: *Are you still there?*

Anthony grabbed the controller from next to him on the bed.

[Anthony]: *Yeah, I was opening one of your pictures. I wanted to see you while we talked.*

It seemed like such a lame thing to say. "Yeah, sorry, I wanted to see your eyes while we talked so I didn't feel like such a fucking loser."

[Jay]: *I have a picture of you open too.*

[Anthony]: *You do? Am I naked? Lol*

[Jay]: *No. But I like those too.*

[Anthony]: *Yeah?*

[Jay]: *God yeah, I jack off all the time thinking about things I want to do with you.*

[Anthony]: *Me too. I wish there were a way we could see each other.*

The screen stayed still for several minutes, and Anthony traced the lines of Jay's face with his fingertips. Finally, the words moved with a new message.

[Jay]: You have a car, right?
[Anthony]: Yeah.
[Jay]: Come see me.
[Anthony]: I can't just come to Detroit. Are you crazy? Where would I stay?
[Jay]: Stay with me. My parents won't care. They barely even notice I'm here. They won't care that you're here.

Anthony stared at the screen, his jaw resting somewhere around his knees. It was crazy. He couldn't just pack up and drive to Detroit. Though now he thought about it, he could have offered Jay the same thing. Jay could stay down there in the basement with him all summer and his parents wouldn't even notice. Once Aaron moved out, they'd found other things to occupy their time. Dad had his pet projects at work and his golf games. Mom had her charities. They didn't need him.

[Anthony]: Your parents aren't going to flip if I just show up?
[Jay]: Nah, they never come down here. And they're at work all day, so we can do whatever we want. ;)
[Anthony]: You want me there?
[Jay]: Every day.

Anthony stared around at the bare cinderblock walls and thick panes of glass on the windows. He'd been underground for so long, light and happiness had become a distant memory. They haunted his dreams and his memories of a time before the world turned dark.

God, he wanted to see the sun again.

[Anthony]: Okay, I'll come. OMG, I will. I'll pack up some stuff, get in my car tomorrow, and come to Detroit.
[Jay]: Really?
[Anthony]: Yeah, where am I going? I'm going to need to print out directions.

ANTHONY

His heart pounded, slamming against the inside of his ribs as he pulled the laptop onto his legs. It took him two tries to reenter his password, but eventually, he brought up Chrome and opened the navigation site. He couldn't do it, leave home with no money and go live with a guy he'd never met. It was insane. Then images of him onstage at his graduation came to mind: standing alone next to the principal, getting that fucking paper, in front of all those people when guys started to yell "faggot" or worse.

He typed his address into the first box.

He typed the address Jay provided into the second box.

Five hours. It would take only five hours to escape, and he could be with Jay. Jay understood him better than anyone did. When she wasn't ignoring him, Anthony's mother battled with him. She hated his hair. She hated his friends. She hated that he wasn't Aaron. Allen had abandoned him, and Aaron, well. Aaron never gave a shit in the first place.

His life would never change. He'd be eighteen in a matter of weeks and had no reason to stay. No hope. No light.

[Anthony]: It will take me 5 hrs.

[Jay]: So when do you think you'll get here?

[Anthony]: If I pack up quickly tonight, my mom should be gone by 11, so I can be there by about 4.

[Jay]: That's perfect. I can't wait to see you!

[Anthony]: I'd better go, it's already 3 and I need to get some sleep before I pack. I'll see you tomorrow afternoon.

[Jay]: That's so awesome. Sleep well, babe. Tomorrow night you'll be sleeping in my bed.

[Anthony]: I can't wait.

Anthony logged off the Xbox and sat back against his pillows. He'd really done it. He'd really planned to leave. His controller dropped to the floor as he set the laptop back between the bed and the dresser. The bottom drawer creaked as he pulled it out and felt around the old socks for one with a distinctive rounded edge of thick glass. It took a minute in the dark, but eventually, he found the sock with his pint of Absolut. For four long years, he'd taken a few swigs out of a bottle before bed to help him fall asleep. Right then, it would take more than a few, keyed up as he was to leave the next day.

As he drank, he imagined Jay's hand caressing his face as he knelt on the floor at a party.

He wouldn't call Anthony a fag.

Their dream lips met, and hope kindled in his chest just as Anthony drifted off into a peaceful sleep.

Chapter Two

Anthony snatched another duffel from his closet and began to shove every pair of underwear he owned into the crevices and rounded corners. He'd packed jeans, T-shirts, and most of the hanging clothes he wanted to take. They lay folded in the big box where he'd always kept his Lego sets. He didn't want Jay to think he was lame, so he dumped the little plastic toys into a garbage bag and threw them in the closet. He couldn't bring himself to throw them out, no matter what his parents decided to do with his room after he left. It took years of birthdays and Christmases to collect them. But the Mustang wouldn't hold a lot.

Almost everything he wanted to take sat in boxes or bags at the bottom of his closet next to the Legos. They stayed hidden from view should someone come into his room.

No one did.

No one bothered to check on him and stop him from packing everything important to him. They didn't care enough to stop him. By eleven o'clock, he'd finished packing, showered, and sat in his room waiting for his mother to leave so he could. He didn't want a confrontation. She would tell him to stay, yell at him until he took his stuff downstairs and unpacked—not because she wanted him to stay, but because she had to be in control.

He almost considered messaging Jay at eleven thirty to let him know about the delay when his mother yelled down the stairs.

"I'm going to the store before I go to the committee meeting. Do you want anything?" She couldn't even be bothered to come all the way downstairs to talk to him. She just yelled at him as if he were the lone lunatic still left in the basement of an asylum.

"No," he yelled back. He didn't need anything. He'd be gone by the time she returned.

"You're almost out of Dr. Pepper," she persisted. "Want me to pick you up a case? It's on sale."

He didn't want to arouse her suspicions, so he shouted back a "Yeah, sure." Maybe someone else would drink it.

Fifteen agonizing minutes later, he finally heard the side door close. He crept up the stairs and watched from behind the blinds in the living room as she backed out of the drive. Fear and excitement warred in him as the tail lights disappeared at the end of the block. She'd be gone a couple of hours, so he had plenty of time, but he ran for the basement stairs anyway.

It took about twenty minutes for him to run up and down the stairs carrying everything that would fit in the car. His heart pounded with anxiety and guilt. He left the furniture, the television, and a bookcase containing most of his paperbacks. He had them all on his phone anyway.

His phone.

Shit.

It killed him that he had to leave it. First, the plan belonged to his parents. More important, if his mother decided to track him, she could do it with his phone. He shredded his soul and deleted all the pictures first. He deleted the texts, removed his email account, and deleted his Facebook app. He left the lock code on, just in case.

Anthony glanced out the window again. When he saw nothing, he turned and headed for the hall. The walk to his parents' room made him paranoid. Every creak of the floor sounded like a person, every bang of a branch on the house like a car door slamming. He turned the knob on their door and went into the one room of the house he never entered. Anthony had no reason to crawl in bed with his parents anymore after a nightmare. He'd stopped doing that when they moved him and Allen to the basement so they could coddle Aaron. It didn't matter that Anthony was terrified of the dark. It didn't matter that for the first year, he thought mice would crawl in bed with him. He'd nearly failed fifth grade because he never slept. They all just said it was because of things happening with Aaron.

Fucking Aaron.

The carpet muffled the sound of his feet as he searched the top of the dresser. If he were going to run, he'd need cash. The hundred bucks he'd hidden away in his own room wouldn't be enough. Whenever he or Allen asked for money for various things, Mom always went to her room to get it. There had to be something in there.

At the opposite end of the dresser, he found a small wooden chest. Carved into the top were a Bible quote and image of footprints in the sand guarding the contents. Great, now Anthony had to worry about God striking him with lightning for stealing, on top of everything else.

He opened the box and pushed aside papers and a watch to find bills underneath. He pulled them out, all of them, and riffled through. About two hundred and fifty dollars would supplement his own hundred and at least let him eat for a while.

A dark voice in the back of his mind reminded Anthony he didn't know Jay. He could be forced to return to DeKalb the next day with his tail between his legs. How would he explain stealing money from his mother to Allen or Aaron? Self-hatred clawed its way through the inside of Anthony's chest, making it hard to breathe. He was a fucking thief and a drug addict, all before he'd turned eighteen. His family must be so proud.

With jerky, shaking hands, he put the money in his pocket, slammed God's little box of guilt, and left the room without so much as a backward glance.

In the kitchen, he looked around his childhood home, the prison that had held him for the last eight years, and sighed. Everyone else had escaped, and now it was his turn. Aaron had moved in with Spencer a few months before, and Allen had gone off to Purdue, coming home less and less often with each passing year.

Anthony pulled a notebook and pen from a rack next to the phone. The fight drained out of him, spilling onto the counter as he stood there trying to figure out how to explain his decision. He started writing again and again, each note ripped from the metal spiral and thrown in the kitchen trash before he signed it. One more try, one more, then he *had* to leave.

Mom & Dad,

You've been telling me for months that if I wanted to live under your roof, I had to go to college. Even Aaron went to college. That's great. Not sure if you noticed, but I'm not Aaron. I'm one of the kids you hid in the basement so you could focus on Aaron. I don't know what it would have taken for you to focus on me, but I'm done trying to guess. I'm done waiting for you to see that I'm still here.

I'm leaving. I have a friend willing to take me in for the summer until I can figure out what to do with my life. My graduation ceremony doesn't mean anything to me. It's just an excuse for the other kids to scream awful things at me like they do at school, so I'm not sticking around for it.

ANTHONY

I just can't do this anymore.
Anthony

His anger seeped into the paper, infusing the ink, searing the words into his heart. He threw the pen on the counter and propped the notebook up against the coffeemaker so his mother wouldn't miss it when she came in.

The walk to the front door seemed longer than necessary, but eventually, he closed it behind him and tested the knob to make sure it locked. A force of habit drilled into him by his mother. Blood roared in his ears as he took the sidewalk to the driveway and climbed into the Mustang loaded down with most of the contents of his bedroom.

The car roared to life and nearly drowned out the little voice in the back of his mind telling him to call it off. He needed only to carry his stuff back in the house, return the money to his parents' room, and rip up the note. Anthony gagged the little voice and backed out of the drive.

By the time he turned out of his subdivision and onto the main road, a sick, giddy nausea had settled into his stomach. No matter how slow he went, the feeling didn't dissipate. He turned into a gas station about a mile from his house and coasted up to the pumps. Inside the station, Anthony grabbed a Coke and a bag of chips and prepaid for gas, all with the cash in his pocket. It felt weird to have that kind of money. He usually carried twenty bucks at the most, since his mother wouldn't let him get a job until he graduated. She said it would interfere with his homework. As if.

Anthony watched the traffic while gas flowed into his old beater. His parents had bought the car for Allen to take him back and forth to school. When Allen went off to college, he left it for Aaron. When Aaron moved out, he left it for Anthony. There was no one else to leave it for, so Anthony took it with him. A pink cement truck passed. Anthony frowned, and it took him a minute or two to realize he was watching for his mother in the traffic. Eventually, she would return from her errands and find the note in the kitchen. Would she look for him? Would she even care he was gone?

The pump handle clicked in his hand, indicating that the flow had ceased—twenty-nine dollars and ninety-five cents. He grinned. At least he wouldn't have to go back in for change. With a full tank of gas, Coke, chips, and the directions he'd printed from the computer, he was ready.

Anthony climbed back into his car, turned it toward the highway, and pulled out smoothly into traffic. The post office lay just ahead and beyond that, the grocery store where his mother shopped for stuff he'd no longer need. Instead, he turned left to avoid it and went past the high school he'd never see again. His heart didn't stop pounding until he merged onto I-88 headed east.

The sun seemed too bright on the cars as they closed in around him. It exhilarated and terrified him to watch the needle on the speedometer climb. The miles ticking away made a giggle threaten to erupt from deep in his chest.

He'd really done it.

He'd left.

The details of the landscape crawled past as one suburb turned into another and the cloudless blue sky stretched out into endless possibilities. Anthony tried to imagine the look on Jay's face when he met him on the doorstep. His eyes would light up, and for once in his life, someone would be happy to see Anthony.

God, he couldn't wait.

ANTHONY

It didn't take long before Anthony rolled down the windows because sweat made him stick to the seat. Wind whipped through his hair, drawing it into his eyes, and he smiled. No more lectures about haircuts. Keeping most of his attention focused on the road, Anthony grabbed a bandana from the bag on the passenger seat and pulled the mess out of his face. He added sunglasses and watched the road stretch out toward his future.

As he merged to get onto I-294, Anthony gave up on silence. He fidgeted with the radio, a custom job Allen put in when he'd had the car. Deep in the back of his heart, he knew if he found a good song, a good sign, a good omen, he'd be okay. It was such a chick thing to do, but he kept punching through programmed stations. On the second to last button, he smiled. Outbreak Monkey was one of his favorite bands. He'd been into them forever, especially since Mackey Sanders came out as gay and told the world if they didn't like it, they could go to hell.

Does it help to say I'm sorry?
That I didn't mean to make you cry?
Does it help if I am truthful
And tell you truly why?
So if I break you, should I fix you?
Will that be a bitter end?
Or maybe just not break you
Just shake hands with my good friend.

The words settled into his heart. He reached into the recesses of his imagination and saw Chase saying them to him. In the afternoon traffic, he could almost hear Chase's voice and maybe even feel the soft touch of a hand on his face. But Chase had broken him and had no intention of fixing things. The hate lingered, and he forced the image in his mind to change. Anthony focused on Jay's gentleness, on Jay's touch, and he relaxed. In just a few hours, he would feel that touch for real.

Anthony Downing, the dreamer of children's dreams.

In the shadow of the biggest city he'd ever seen, Anthony swung onto I-94 East, where he would stay for the next two hundred plus miles. He watched the tall buildings in the distance and wondered if Detroit would swallow him up like Chicago might if he just turned north instead of continuing east. If only Allen lived near Chicago instead of Aaron, he might have put on his turn signal. But Aaron would send him back to his parents with a lecture on college. None of them fucking asked if he *wanted* to go to college. They didn't care what he did with his life as long as they wouldn't have to foot the bill.

He couldn't tell them that he had no fucking clue. Maybe staying with Jay and getting away from the weight of his family's expectations would help him figure it out.

By the time he reached the Indiana border, his head hurt. He hadn't slept well the night before, and keeping the radio loud enough to hear over the wind didn't help. The air hadn't worked in the Mustang since long before he'd gotten it, and the day scorched outside his windows.

A sign on the side of the road caught his attention. He was coming up on I-65 to Indianapolis. One quick turn and he could be on his way to see Allen. Allen, the brother who had always been there for him, always protected him—until one day, he wasn't. He'd left Anthony to navigate the horrifying, shark-infested waters of high school as the skinny, effeminate, gay kid brother of a lunatic. Yeah, that went well.

Besides, Allen would be pissed when he found out Anthony stole money from their parents. Allen lived and died by their mother's approval. He'd assume Anthony had stolen it for a fix. Everyone would. When he came home from rehab, he'd ceased being Anthony and just turned into the junkie down the hall.

Anthony moved into the left lane, determined not to catch the exit to Allen's when it appeared. His heart broke a little when he drove past it. It broke a little more at the sign for a college called Purdue North Central. He remembered all of them together taking Allen down to Purdue and how his heart hardened all the way home because Allen had left him.

Well, now it was his turn to leave.

The road droned on, mile after mile, until he reached a sign that took away some of the sting in his heart. Across the endless forest of trees, a blue oasis of a sign read: *Welcome to Pure Michigan*. He didn't know what was so pure about it, but the sign made his tired back not so sore.

Just two hundred thirty-five more miles to Detroit.

He nearly exited the highway at one point, because the idea of a Chocolate Garden called to him, but Anthony stayed his course. The sheer number of signs for wineries, distilleries, and breweries made him wonder if he'd entered a state full of alcoholics—maybe he *was* home. One song melded into the next like the miles of the highway surrounded by trees, grass, and cracks in the asphalt. He wished about a hundred times for his phone so he could either listen to one of his playlists or check out what was happening on Facebook. Did they know he was gone yet? Did they care?

Anthony learned many things down the next stretch of highway. In Decatur, he learned if he popped a piece of gum from the foil package hard enough, it would bounce off the steering wheel and fly out the window. He waited for the ten-car pileup from the errant piece of gum, but it didn't happen. About ten miles later, he figured out there was fucking nothing but trees between Chicago and Detroit. In Paw Paw, he learned Walmart had taken over the planet with all of their cloned stores selling cloned T-shirts with interchangeable sports teams. He learned you're seriously bored when Sprinkle Road makes you giggle. But, in Oshtemo, he watched the forest green disappear in a shower of white clouds and blue skies as far as he could see. The world seemed bigger then, far too big for Anthony to be able to navigate alone.

Okay, the Climax highway sign made him laugh too.

The sunset behind him contrasted with the vibrant horizon: a sky bruised with dusky clouds, farmhouses peeking through the trees, and the shells of dead truck tires scattered like shrapnel of a forgotten road war. The serene picture occupied his mind, and he zoned out for a few miles. That's when he almost missed the cars stopped on the highway. His heart thundered against the sudden surge of adrenaline in his blood, and he slammed on the brakes, narrowly avoiding the Kia Sportage in front of him. The driver in his rearview mirror laid on the horn, but at least he didn't hear the screech of metal against metal.

Creeping a little to the left, Anthony glimpsed lots of red-and-blue flashing lights and a long line of cars in front of the Sportage. There must be some kind of accident. The clock on the dash showed it was about half past two in his own time zone. He'd forgotten all about the time zone change crossing into Michigan when he talked to Jay, so he was supposed to be there in half an hour. He'd never make it. But it wasn't like Jay would leave. It was his house. Anthony would just be late.

The clock continued to tick away the time as he sat, unmoving, behind the Sportage with its annoyingly complete stick family frolicking across the back. The lack of air moving through the window made sweat drip down his back as he shifted in the seat. After he hadn't moved in ten solid minutes, he reached into a backpack on the passenger seat and grabbed his paperback copy of *Harry Potter and the Deathly Hallows*. He couldn't stand to sit there and do nothing. Each time Anthony read a line, he glanced up to check the stalled traffic and grew more anxious. Nothing from the pages stuck in his mind as his eyes swept past them with zero attention to the words.

Time passed at the same speed as the crawling traffic.

The car lurched as he tapped the gas to move up another car length. A solid thunk under his hood troubled him, but the car glided forward and he kept pace with the other cars, diverting to the right to get around the accident. When he finally saw the cop directing traffic, Anthony noticed everyone veering off the freeway onto an exit ramp. Panic gripped his throat, choking him. The directions said to stay on the highway. If he got off, he wouldn't know how to find Jay's place. He didn't have a phone to rerun the GPS directions and no Wi-Fi to check on the computer.

The cop left him no choice; he followed the other cars merging to form one line as they crept along the edge of the highway. He lost the Sportage in the mass exodus but managed to slide in behind a silver Mercury Sable with a broken tail light. A faded sign indicated they were getting off at Route 23 North.

He followed the herd until he reached the light at the top of the hill. His car kicked again as he put his foot on the gas, hesitating before it moved forward, so Anthony coasted into a gas station to see if his printed map would give him an alternative route back to I-94 and on to Detroit. The font was almost too small to read, but he slid his finger up Route 23 until he found I-96, which would take him back to I-94, and then he could find Jay's and everything would be okay.

Only, when he reached I-96, he found it shut down due to construction. In a disturbing lack of light, he pulled out the map again and tried to find yet another route. He proceeded north on Route 23 and eventually turned onto I-75 and found I-696. The car continued to slip, sometimes catching on a gear. At one point, he considered pulling off and calling someone, but he didn't have anyone to call. He only had an email address for Jay and no way of sending a message without Wi-Fi or a cell phone.

Anthony studied the signs as they passed, trying to decide where to come off I-696 to get gas. After all the miles traveled and the extra hours stuck in traffic, the needle hovered a whispered prayer above empty. If only he'd topped off in that little Shell station, he might have made it all the way to Jay's, but as the car knocked again, he gave in to the need. Woodward Avenue sounded like a good place. Mr. Woodward had been his high school English teacher, one of the only people who actually cared if he showed up. It was a sign, a very good sign.

He coasted to the pump at the Sunoco and went inside to pay. Twenty bucks should see him through the last few miles to Jay's place. Anthony started to get excited again, but nervous because he was so late. It was nearly ten o'clock now. The construction and accident traffic had fucked him sideways, and the time change certainly didn't help.

He didn't bother with snacks this time. As soon as he finished pumping gas and got back into the car, he turned toward Woodward and the lanes of traffic that would get him to the turnaround back toward I-696. A shuddering worried him, and when he hit the gas, nothing happened. Almost thirty seconds later, much to the dismay of oncoming traffic, the Mustang shot out across Woodward as the gear caught. He swerved into the far lane, and when he tried to merge back, the car gave out altogether. It was all he could do to get it into the small parking lot in front of him. The car coasted sideways across a couple of the farthest spaces, out of the way of other cars that might pull in.

He glanced up at the building. Mears Liquors. Even with the lights off, he could read the sign. Appropriate, it'd be a liquor store. It seemed weird for it to be closed so early, but then he realized it was Sunday.

He tried the car again, but when he put it into reverse and stepped on the gas, the engine only revved. His dreams and his escape died a slow, painful death under the hood of his car.

ANTHONY

Icy sweat rolled down his back in the cooling evening air. He had no idea what the fuck had happened to the car or what he should do. Jay wouldn't be able to find him because he couldn't call. His parents probably weren't even looking for him, and he'd had about two hours sleep the night before. His eyes hurt from the strain, his head hurt from the rapid influx of adrenaline, and most of all, his soul hurt with a terrible kind of ache.

Anthony climbed out of the car and searched the shadows clinging to the edges of the parking lot. He didn't see a pay phone or any signs that someone remained in the store. The buildings on either side were dark. His balls crept a little higher at the thought of sleeping alone in his car, but he didn't have many options. It probably cost a lot of money to get a hotel room, and he didn't even know where to find a hotel.

With no one to help him, and no plan, Anthony swiped the bottom of his T-shirt over the wetness on his face, which he told himself was just sweat. He pushed the front seats of the Mustang forward, climbed into the narrow backseat, and lay down facing the front so he could see if anyone tried to fuck with him. The stifling car felt like a tomb with the windows closed, but the thought of leaving them open terrified Anthony. Instead, he double-checked the locks on the doors, pounded his backpack into something resembling the shape of a pillow, and broke his neck to lay on it.

An unmerciful battalion of crickets surrounded him, crawling on the edges of his imagination. Somewhere nearby, a door slammed. A dog barked his disapproval. All the sounds of the city lay a fraction of an inch from him. A faulty layer of iron and glass became his only protection from the world.

In the blackness of an unfamiliar city, on the edge of fear, Anthony wrapped thin arms around his chest and closed his eyes, desperate for sleep to chase away his demons.

Chapter Three

Brendan Mears scowled at the digitized image of the car sitting in the lot. He'd been watching it on his screen for hours, waiting for it to move. Something about it bugged him, and anger ate at his nerves because Patrick wouldn't text him back. Again. The car looked abandoned, but he knew, just as soon as Patrick checked it out, some lunatic with a gun would throw open the door and blow his brother's face off. Then Patrick would be faceless and he'd never get a date—all because liquor stores and desperate men made bad combinations.

Brendan should just call the cops and get it over with, but they thought he was fucking crazy, just like everyone else. They wouldn't help. He watched, helpless, as his brother, the only person he had left in his miserable goddamned life, pulled into the lot.

Fuck it.

He dialed Patrick's cell and let it ring again and again until the line connected.

"There's a beater in the parking lot. Don't go near it. It's been there all fucking night." He grumbled out the words in a long string before Patrick had a chance to say anything. A long pause followed, and then sarcasm permeated the morning.

"It's seven o'clock in the morning. Don't you ever sleep?"

A slow, hot rage burned in Bren, filling what was left inside him with embers. For the last two years it had been like a lover, wrapped around him at night as he slept, whispering to him in the darkness. Bren didn't think he had another mood anymore. Rage filled the hollowness in his bones.

"No. I don't fucking sleep."

"Okay." Patrick dragged out the word. "So have you run the playback? Is it a junkie or something?"

"Don't go near it, Patrick. Just call the cops."

"I'm sick of cops. Just check the damn history."

"Fine," Bren snapped. "But stay in the goddamned car."

"Yes, little brother."

That rankled Bren's already prickled nerves. He grabbed the Area 51 mug from the counter, a gag gift he'd gotten for their father before the world went to shit. Two mouthfuls of coffee laced with a heavy-handed dose of Bailey's helped to steady his hands. It took a minute for the browser to load the store's historical surveillance. Patrick stayed quiet, and for that, Bren thanked... well, not God, but something.

Everything between them seemed to result in a fight lately. He could hear more weariness in his brother's voice with each call. It wouldn't be long before Patrick gave up on the broken mess keeping him chained to a life he didn't want.

"Looks like it rolled in about ten last night, just after the store closed." Bren studied the video playback. "Damn, from the camera angle, I can't tell in the dark, but it looks like a vintage Mustang. An '85 maybe."

"Dude, I don't care if it's a Corvette. Who the hell is in it?"

Bren rolled his eyes. "A Corvette is a Chevy, a Mustang is a Ford. God, you're hopeless." He leaned closer. "I can't get a good look at the driver. It's not going very fast, like the thing barely made it into the space. Wait, the door is opening." Bren watched as a small, thin figure tumbled out of the car and had the good manners to turn his anguished face to the camera. Bren zoomed in and saw pixelated tears on the boy's cheeks.

"Oh damn...."

"What?"

ANTHONY

"It's a kid, Pat. Can't be more than sixteen or seventeen. He got out, looked around, wiped his eyes on his shirt, and crawled into the back. He's probably still asleep." Bren leaned back from the computer. "Just call the cops, man. Let them deal with him."

"You're telling me there's a runaway kid in our parking lot, and I should just send him back to whatever fresh hell he ran from?"

Bren held himself back from yelling, just barely. "I'm telling you it's not your problem."

"Neither is running the store."

Bren hit the End button and slammed the phone down, cutting off the rebuke in his brother's voice. Fuck him. Patrick didn't know a goddamn thing about it. He didn't have the fucking nightmares, that day burned into the back of his eyelids like laser-engraved misery.

Bren added enough booze to the mug to make his coffee look more like chocolate milk.

Fucking Patrick.

Chapter Four

Patrick wished for a very long moment that he could have taken back the last bit. Bren didn't need his angst; he already had enough for both of them. He took another long sip of his coffee, working up the nerve to go get the kid out of his lot. The day had already started to take on a heat haze. If he left the guy in the car, it would be a hundred degrees in there by the time he woke up. Patrick sighed and put his travel mug back in the cup holder.

At five foot nine with a video-gamer body, he wasn't likely to scare anyone into doing what he wanted. Bren had always been the big one. Six foot one with broad shoulders, muscled arms, and a wicked left hook. Well, until the only thing he started hitting was a bottle. Damn it, maybe being thirty would finally work to Patrick's advantage. Besides, he'd had a baby brother for most of his life. Surely he'd learned to intimidate someone, right?

Yeah, and maybe the rabbit would finally get some Trix.

Patrick slammed the door on his father's RAV4, the one he couldn't quite bring himself to either sell or call his own yet, and started across the lot. He didn't see any movement, no life inside the car. Feeling ridiculous at being scared to bang on the window of a teenage boy's car, he pulled his balls out of his pocket and stepped up next to the harbinger of doom. He kept the cell phone in his hand, ready to call 9-1-1 at any sign of trouble, and peeked inside. Damn it, life didn't used to be this hard.

The sight in the backseat stopped him short.

Bren had nailed it. The boy couldn't have been more than sixteen or seventeen. A shock of brown hair framed an angelic face, anxious even in sleep. His body curled in on itself, protective, like a frightened animal. He clutched at the jacket spread over him like a lifeline and used a bright orange backpack as a pillow. Discarded Coke bottles and chip bags littered the front seat, as though he'd just come off a road trip. The windows weren't even cracked; the kid had to be burning up.

Before he could lose his shit, Patrick banged hard on the window. The boy shot upright, slamming his head on the side of the car just above his backpack pillow. He rubbed the back of it and searched his surroundings until his eyes met Patrick's. They were shadowed, wide, and terrified.

Patrick made a motion asking the boy to roll down the window, but he just shook his head and scooted as far as he could away from the side where Patrick stood. All of the anger, fear, and frustration drained out of Patrick as he saw a young Bren sitting in that backseat, terrified of the world.

"I'm not going to hurt you. This is my store." Patrick spoke loudly to be heard through the glass. "Do you need help?"

The boy inside the car blinked and stared around again, as if searching for someone to make the decision for him. Finally, after what seemed like a very long time, he leaned forward. At first, Patrick thought he might be throwing up, but he just put on his shoes. Then, he climbed up on the driver's-side seat, which was folded down and shoved all the way forward against the steering wheel. He popped the door lock, jerked the handle, and pushed hard on the door.

Patrick backed up to give him room, his hands up in a gesture of calm. The boy stepped out of the car and threw his jacket back on top of his backpack. Patrick's heart ached as he wondered if it was all the kid had in the world.

"Can I use the john?" The boy kept close to the car, his bravado completely out of line with his posture. It looked as if he might dive back in at a moment's provocation.

"Sure, let me get my stuff out of the car and I'll unlock the door. You're not going to kill me, are you?" He'd meant it as a joke, but the way the kid's eyes widened and darted back toward the car, he wished he hadn't said it at all. "I'm kidding, kid."

The boy didn't say anything else. He simply followed Patrick, keeping a distance of several feet between them as they ventured toward the front door. The phone in his pocket started to ring—Bren no doubt ready to scream at him for letting the kid in the store alone with him. But really, his companion weighed maybe a hundred and twenty pounds with shoes. Patrick couldn't articulate to his brother that he'd just found a younger version of Bren in the backseat of a junk car. Bren would hate him for the reminder that he acted like a scared little boy.

Once they were inside, Patrick locked the door behind them so no one else would come in before he opened the store to customers. Drunks wanted their morning fix just as soon as they could get it. They'd just have to wait. The boy's hands trembled as Patrick walked him down the whiskey aisle toward the coolers and then back into the stockroom. He noticed that Kevin had done a great job getting the coolers stocked the night before. Finally. He didn't want to have another talk with the guy.

He hated being the boss. He never wanted to be the boss—that was Bren's job. Unfortunately, shit just never worked out the way you planned.

"The john is that door right there. Just come back up to the front when you're done."

"Sure."

Patrick sighed and returned to the front counter. He hated being in the store alone. Even after they'd cleaned everything, even though he'd been an entire state away, the ghosts of the robbery clung to every inch the space. The bloodstains lingered in his imagination. Fuck. He'd rather be anywhere but here, but he didn't want to compound the kid's terror by hovering over him. Even if the kid stole a pint in those loose jeans, he probably needed it more than someone who actually had the money to pay for it.

Lost in his thoughts, Patrick didn't hear the door open in the back, but movement caught his eye and he watched the boy shuffle up the aisle. You'd think it was the Green Mile and he marched toward his execution.

"Your car die?" Patrick cut to the chase. He wanted to draw more than just one or two stuttered syllables at a time.

"You think?" the kid shot back, but when Patrick glared at him, he dropped his gaze. "It starts, but it doesn't go anywhere."

"You *can* talk, and you have an attitude, fabulous." He smiled at the boy, and while he didn't get a smile in return, the idea seemed to be there.

"I can. I can even read and do math and stuff."

"What does math have to do with—?"

"It's from *Harry Potter*." The boy started to shut down again, as though maybe what little bravado he'd found in the bathroom dissipated in his fear. Patrick smiled, trying for gentle instead of patronizing.

"I haven't read it."

"It's my favorite."

"What's your name, kid?"

"Anthony."

"I'm Patrick. This was my dad's store until a few years ago, and I guess now it's mine. How did you end up in my parking lot?"

Anthony shrugged and began to rearrange the bottles on the counter with black-nailed fingers. Patrick waited. He'd had a lot of experience lately dealing with reticent people; Bren seemed to be the definition of it. Two years and he still hadn't made it out the front door of his own house.

After a few minutes, the blueberry vodka sat with others of its kind. The grape came next, and then orange and raspberry. Not only had Anthony lined them up, but he did it in alphabetical order. Patrick couldn't even get his own staff to be that conscientious.

"I left my parents' house to stay with a friend in Detroit." Anger welled in the soft spaces between Anthony's words.

"That tells me how you ended up in Detroit with Illinois plates," Patrick replied. "But not why you're in my parking lot."

"I told you, there's something wrong with my fucking car."

"You don't have a cell phone?" Patrick asked. Didn't everybody have a cell phone these days, especially angry, entitled children?

"No."

"Do you want to call your friend and have him pick you up?"

"I... no." The bravado slipped again, exposing a soft vulnerability Patrick hated almost as much as the anger. But, Jesus, it was like pulling teeth with this kid. Frustration knotted the muscles in the back of his neck, and he closed his eyes before letting out a slow breath. When he opened them again, the kid stared at him with wide-eyed fear. The contrast startled him.

"I don't know his phone number," the kid whispered as if revealing a deep, dark secret.

Patrick stared, incredulous. "Let me get this straight. You jumped in the car and drove at least, what, five or six hours to meet some guy you don't even know well enough to have a phone number for. Is that it?"

Anthony looked away, misery deepening the lines in his face.

"How old are you?"

"I'll be eighteen in a couple weeks."

"Christ, the phone is right there. Call your parents."

At that, Anthony spun on his heel and ran for the door as though he'd been waiting for an excuse since he'd come through it. The door rattled in the frame as he shook it. Tears streamed down his pale cheeks, and something in Patrick broke. He didn't go to Anthony right away, unable to stand the sight of his pain. Everything in the boy reminded him of that awful day, the day he saw the life leave his brother's eyes. The day they stood together and put their father in the ground.

Instead, he picked up the store phone and dialed a number almost as familiar as his own.

"Patrick?" the bleary voice asked in a panic. Apparently, not everyone he knew got up before eight.

"Oh, shit, Sandy, I'm sorry. I forgot it was so early. It's been…. Can you do me a favor, uhm, later? Maybe when your eyes are open?"

The silence from the other end of the phone felt like a physical weight. She wouldn't stay mad at him for long, but while she was, it would be painful.

"You woke me up out of a sound sleep to ask me for a favor… later?"

"Sandy, I'll take you out for the best sushi in the city. I'm so sorry." Patrick rubbed the back of his neck. "When I got to the store this morning, I found a kid in my parking lot. It's been a long day already, and it's barely eight o'clock."

"A kid? What do you mean?"

"I mean a seventeen-year-old boy."

"Is he okay?" The concern in her voice warmed him.

"Physically, I think. Look, his car is broken down, and I was wondering if you'd come and take a look. Bren said it's a 1985 Mustang."

"It's a 1986," Anthony said miserably from the door. At least he'd stopped trying to get through the glass.

"The kid says it's a 1986."

"Yeah, let me get a shower and I'll bring the truck by to check it out before I open up the garage. Where are his parents?"

"Illinois, I'd have to guess by the plates. He hasn't been very forthcoming about why he's here," Patrick said the last with a long look at Anthony, who seemed to be studying the advertisements in the window.

"I'll be there about ten."

"Thanks, Sandy. Dinner is on me."

"Nah, I can't turn away a kid in trouble."

"I know, which is why dinner is on me."

Patrick hung up the phone after they said their good-byes, and turned to Anthony, who hadn't moved from in front of the door. The kid's clothes weren't torn or even too worn, and he scuffed a battered tennis shoe against the floor as he picked at something on his jeans. He looked clean and healthy, probably not physically abused. He hadn't limped or winced as he came into the store.

The prospect of sexual abuse flitted across Patrick's mind. The boy was beautiful and sensitive. Something solidified in his gut at the thought. *Please God, don't let it be that.*

"Where does your friend live? I'm guessing you didn't drive all the way out here without an address?"

Anthony dug into the back pocket of his jeans. He pulled out a couple of folded sheets of paper and handed them over. Patrick opened the papers with one last glance at Anthony and found Google Maps directions from DeKalb, Illinois, to an address in Detroit. Patrick followed the directions in his head and looked up sharply at Anthony.

"Did he tell you this was his house?"

"I... I think so, he said to come there."

"Kid, this is a business district. How old is your friend?"

"Seventeen, like me."

"We've got a bit before I have to open the store or Sandy gets here to check out your car. Why don't we go check it out?" He thought of something else. "Are you hungry?"

"Yeah."

"When did you eat last?"

"I had breakfast at home yesterday, chips and stuff in the car."

"Jesus." Patrick shook his head. "Come on. Let's hit a McDonald's and then check out your friend's address. Okay?"

Anthony didn't move. Tension vibrated through his thin frame as he regarded Patrick with resigned fear.

"Why are you helping me? What.... What do you want?"

Patrick blew out a heavy breath and tried to force the words in his head to make sense.

"You remind me of the kid my little brother used to be, and I don't want you to turn into him."

Anthony's eyes widened, but Patrick just stomped out from behind the counter, pulling his keys out in the process. He left the coffee mug and paper and took only his wallet. To his credit, Anthony didn't bolt when Patrick opened the door. He did, however, move quickly through it, leaving Patrick to follow as he went to the Mustang and pulled out the orange backpack.

It took a long time for Anthony to walk from the Mustang to the RAV4. Patrick could see the indecision in each step. Anthony shouldn't trust him, not a complete stranger. Everyone knew what happened when you trusted a stranger. Unfortunately, desperation compromises the choices of reasonable people, even seventeen-year-old kids. With no options, Anthony reached the SUV and caught Patrick's gaze with resignation.

"Come on." Patrick unlocked the doors and they both climbed in, determined.

"What happened to your brother?" Anthony asked as Patrick put his key in the ignition and started the truck.

"He was shot." Patrick pulled smoothly out of the space and pointed the front of the truck toward the road.

"I'm sorry."

"Yeah, me too. It sucks when someone comes and steals your life away."

"I know how that feels."

Patrick looked sharply at Anthony, but the boy didn't say anything else. He merely watched Woodward Avenue go by as they followed it up toward Detroit.

Anthony didn't talk on the twenty-minute ride. The bags under his eyes could have held most of the contents of the backpack he clung to. He didn't throw it in the backseat, or even let it rest in the floorboard of the truck. He wrapped his arms around it as if the nylon fabric held the secrets of the universe.

The GPS instructions led them to the part of Lafayette overlooking I-75, and Patrick double-checked the screen when they found nothing but a rundown four-story building.

"The destination is on your left."

"You have arrived."

But where? Anthony sat forward, his face a mask of mute horror as Patrick pulled in through iron gates to a small parking lot next to a broken-down building. Patrick couldn't imagine what it must look like in the dead of night, which is when Anthony would have reached it. It didn't make sense that this was where a seventeen-year-old boy would choose to meet a friend.

"Have you ever met this guy before?" Patrick slid the RAV into a spot near the front. He didn't want to leave his car in the lot, but he wanted to see what kind of place it was.

"No. We met over Xbox."

"What were you going to do when you got here?"

"I... I thought I was coming to his house. He invited me to stay the summer. I don't know what's happening." Fear warred with hostility in Anthony's voice, like a child trying to be a grown-up but not quite finding the right tenor.

"Okay, well, let's go see what this place is. Maybe he works here or something. Do you have a picture of him?"

Anthony unzipped a small pocket on the front of the backpack and removed a folded piece of paper. He opened it slowly, revealing an inkjet photo of a teenage boy. Patrick took the picture and studied it. The boy looked around Anthony's age, with sandy-brown hair and a pretty face laced with fear and sadness. He appeared to be in a backyard somewhere surrounded by faded, low-resolution grass.

"What's his name?"

"Jay. James Marshall."

Patrick nearly said he'd bet the RAV4 it wasn't, but he stayed quiet. Instead, he pulled the door handle and climbed out of the truck. Anthony followed, backpack swung over his shoulder.

"Hey." Patrick kept his voice low and soothing. "We don't know what we're going to find here. Why don't you leave the backpack in the truck? If he's here, we can come back out and get it."

Anthony hesitated. He fisted the shoulder strap and took a step back. Long, wary lines of anxiety crossed his forehead. His gaze darted from the fence between the lot and the highway to the gate.

"Anthony. I'm not going to hurt you. I'm trying to help you. Something isn't right here."

"Yeah, and I look like your brother. I know."

Patrick suppressed a sigh. "Let's just go check it out. Then we'll go back to your car and you can figure out what you want to do. We didn't come all the way out here just to fight over this."

ANTHONY

Anthony opened the door of the RAV4, threw his backpack onto the seat, and slammed the door a little too hard. Patrick closed his eyes in silent prayer for a moment before hitting the fob to lock the truck. Then he took the lead toward the gate and led Anthony to the front of the building.

It was a bookstore.

"Maybe Jay works here." Anthony's voice held a little more hope than Patrick would have mustered. He opened the door and let Anthony lead the way up the first flight of stairs. Glancing to his left, he saw a sign that said "no photography and no bags." Well, at least he'd managed to convince Anthony to leave his backpack in the car. Patrick breathed in the heavy smell of musty books and old paper. It was nothing like the new-book smell at a retail store, more like the dusty stacks at school. He missed it.

A beautiful younger black woman stood behind the counter talking to an older Middle Eastern guy in a COEXIST T-shirt made up of seemingly random symbols. As Patrick approached, he recognized a couple of them as images from *Doctor Who*. The woman smiled at them and held up a finger while she finished with her sci-fi fan.

Books, toys, and comics littered the back of the counter around several old adding machines. Patrick leaned against the counter and turned toward the larger part of the room, where dozens of huge bookshelves made small pathways through the space, like library shelves but taller. The books in the front rows were old leather tomes under glass, and Patrick couldn't imagine what they were. He wanted to go take a look but waited for the clerk behind the counter so they could find out about the kid.

The *Doctor Who* fan wandered off, and the woman turned to Anthony.

"Well, hello there, young man. How can I help you?" She smiled at him, the pale gold tank top she wore reflecting gold specks in her eyes.

"Do you know this guy?" Anthony cut to the chase as he held up the image he'd kept close in his pocket. The women pulled a heavy pair of glasses from the counter and put them on one-handed while holding the opened paper. She studied it for nearly a minute, almost as if she traced the contours of his face with her gaze. Her head shook as she handed it back.

"I'm sorry, I've not seen him in here. At least, not that I remember."

"He doesn't work here?"

"No, he definitely doesn't work here."

Anthony's shoulders slumped and he bowed his head for just a moment before thanking her.

"Do you want to look around?" Patrick asked him.

"I don't know. I don't know what to do." The words shook in his desperate fear. He looked so much like a boy then, not the tough, angry kid on the edge of manhood. Patrick put a hand on his shoulder, and for once, Anthony didn't look as though he wanted to throw it off. The anguish in his expression hurt Patrick's soul.

"Let's look around and see if he's here or if anyone has seen him. Then we'll pick up breakfast and go back to see about your car. After that, we'll just take things one step at a time. Okay?"

They checked each of the remaining three floors systematically. The subsequent floors looked the same as the one above. They ran across a few employees, each sitting on a footstool in the aisle reshelving books, each of them with a walkie-talkie, and each of them with no information on the boy in the picture.

After the better part of an hour, Patrick put an arm around Anthony's shoulder and guided him to the door.

"I don't understand," Anthony whispered as they walked down the few steps between the first floor and the front door.

"I don't either, Anthony," Patrick admitted. "Let's just get some food and go back to the store."

The walk to the car seemed so much longer with Anthony dragging his feet and scraping the soles along the gravel drive. When they reached the truck, Patrick disengaged the locks and Anthony climbed in, pulling his backpack to his chest and wrapping thin arms around it. He didn't try to engage in any kind of conversation but stared listlessly through the window at the highway passing below the truck.

Patrick didn't try to pull him from his thoughts until they reached a fast-food place about ten minutes from the store. He pulled into the drive-thru behind three other cars and turned to Anthony.

"What would you like? It's on me this morning."

"I should pay for your breakfast to thank you for the wasted trip to Grandpa Bob's Giant Creepy Bookstore." Anthony pulled a battered wallet from his backpack.

"Actually, it's Creepy Bob's Ancient Book Emporium," Patrick replied. "And put that away. I have a feeling things may get worse before they get better. Keep your money, Anthony, you may need it."

"Thanks."

"Now, what kind of heart-attack-inducing item would you like from the breakfast menu? We have a coronary on a muffin, bypass on a bagel, or I think we may even have a strokerritto with sausage and peppers."

Anthony choked back a snort. "Strokerritto?"

"Yeah, I was trying too hard, wasn't I?"

"Kinda. It sounds like a porn flick." Anthony raised an eyebrow at Patrick, who chortled in an uncomfortable "I'm not a perv, I swear" kind of way.

"Fine. I'm having two coronary muffins. I think I'll stay away from the strokerritto." The car in front of them moved up, and Patrick followed. The sun beat down through the driver's-side window. He rolled down the glass barrier and soaked up its warmth. Even in early June, summer seemed to be in full swing, and Patrick couldn't get enough.

"Oh, I'm totally going with two strokerrittos, and a diabetes-inducing giant Coke, with hot sauce please." Anthony smiled, and Patrick decided he'd much rather see that expression than the broken one the kid had been wearing since he'd found the car.

"You want hot sauce in a Coke? You are a strange little thing, aren't you?"

"No, that's not what I—" Anthony stopped as Patrick sat smirking at him. "Funny guy."

"Nope, not even a little." Patrick laughed and moved up again until they were the next ones in line.

"Thank you for doing this, Patrick."

"What? Feeding you junk food?"

"When my car decided it didn't want to go anywhere last night and I realized I had nowhere to go, I… I was so scared. I'm still scared, but thanks for making things seem not so awful for a while."

"You sure you don't want to call your parents?"

"I may have to, but no, I don't want to." The light and joy in Anthony's eyes extinguished just as fast as it had come with their joking conversation. The anger returned, a rage barely contained in the boy's quiet features. Patrick wanted the smile back because Bren had the same fucking look he now saw on Anthony's younger face. He'd had it for two years now, and Patrick wondered if it had become permanent.

The car in front of them moved before Patrick had a chance to say anything, so he rolled forward to the speaker and put in their orders, making sure to remember the hot sauce for Anthony. On impulse, he added a couple of apple pies. Hard to be unhappy in the presence of apple pie, right?

ANTHONY

They were silent for the ten minutes it took to get back to the store. Anthony didn't take his food out of the bag; he didn't even pop the straw from the paper. He simply sat and watched the little town of Ferndale, Michigan, pass outside the window until they turned into the parking lot. The sight of Anthony's car elicited a disgusted snort, and Patrick wondered if it had more to do with the fact it hadn't disappeared or that it couldn't move.

"Let's take the food into the store and eat at the counter," Patrick suggested after they climbed out of the truck. He wanted to forestall any arguments about Anthony sitting in the car until Sandy got there to check it out. Something deep in his gut didn't want Anthony to be alone. Bren spent too much fucking time alone.

The kid shrugged and followed him into the store, where they sat at the front counter and ate quietly while they waited for Sandy. It took less time than Patrick expected. Around nine thirty, a huge tow truck pulled into the lot and stopped behind the crippled Mustang. Anthony's eyes widened as he stared out the store's plate-glass windows.

"Are they going to take my car?" The defeated anguish in Anthony's tone made Patrick walk over and put a hand on his shoulder as they stood watching the truck.

"That's my friend Sandy. We went to high school together. She's a mechanic, and I asked her to come and take a look at your car. See if she could get it working."

"What, are you going for sainthood or something?"

Patrick had to smile at that. "Yep. Come on." He squeezed Anthony's shoulder before dropping his hand away. "I'll take you to meet her."

Anthony led the way as they headed outside but then he stood back, away from the truck, and waited for Patrick to approach Sandy first. Her sleeveless T-shirt exposed sharp, vivid tattoos and the muscled biceps of a woman who spent her days pulling apart cars. She'd pushed her spiky, black hair back with a worn red bandana, and her ice-blue eyes bored into them both. The whole package of Sandra Caldwell scared the piss out of grown men. Too bad for Anthony he didn't know she was harmless as a kitten.

"Thanks for coming." Patrick pulled her into a hug.

"Can't turn down a lost kid," she said, keeping her eyes on Anthony as Patrick drew back.

A grin broke across Patrick's face. "Oh, so I could be dead on the side of the highway, then?"

"Depends. You got Triple-A?"

Patrick snorted and pulled Anthony forward. "This is Anthony. I found him in my parking lot this morning. Anthony, say hi to Sandy."

"Hi to Sandy."

"Oh, I like this one." Sandy's fierce grin brought a slight smile to Anthony's face. "Okay, tell me about the car."

"I... I drove here from just outside of Chicago. It started slipping out of gear some and then got worse when I pulled off here to get gas. I turned around in that cut-over thing there"—he pointed to the small turning lane off Woodward Avenue—"and it caught one last time, and then I heard a loud noise and coasted into the parking lot. I tried the gas after that, but it just revved and nothing happened."

"Shit." Sandy shook her head. "That sounds like a blown transmission. I'm going to need to take it back to the garage and take a look." She gave Patrick a meaningful look over Anthony's head. If her diagnosis proved true, it would be expensive. He read every dollar sign of it in her gaze.

"Do you have anything in there you need?" she asked Anthony, who stood looking shell-shocked and empty. "Kid?"

"Sorry, I.... Everything I own is in that car."

"Okay," Patrick stepped in. "There's an apartment above the store I use for storage. You and your stuff can stay up there until we can figure out what's up with your car. It may be at the garage for a few days." Patrick returned Sandy's look and read the word *weeks* across her lips. The kid probably didn't have a dime, so if he refused to call his parents, he'd be around for a while.

Shit. He'd just adopted a teenager.

Chapter Five

"I can do the labor for free, but a new tranny is going to cost between eight hundred and a thousand dollars. While I was under there, I also noticed you needed new rotors and pads on your brakes. They're shot to fuck. I can't believe someone let you drive around like that. So, with tax and shipping, we're probably looking at twelve hundred for a rough estimate."

Sandy's words a few hours later dropped a car-shaped bomb onto Anthony's life. He watched his options flitter away in the early afternoon light.

"I'd... I.... Jesus." He took a long, slow breath and leaned hard against the liquor store counter as the room shifted beneath him. "I don't have that kind of money. I don't want to call my parents. I just... I can't."

He stood up and wandered to the display window at the front of the store, staring out over the parking lot and the street beyond. He'd emailed Jay from the computer in Patrick's office, but in the two hours since, he hadn't heard a word. Was he hurt? Sick? Did his parents find out about their plan and put him on lockdown? Was he abducted by aliens? Anthony could use a little help right about now. Aliens didn't sound like such a bad idea—way better than calling the parents he'd stolen from, the ones who had his life all planned out whether he wanted to live it or not. The parents who'd left him in the basement until he could no longer stand the transparent bars on the windows.

"Look." Sandy planted her hands on her hips. "We'll leave it in the lot at the shop until you decide what you want to do. It'll be locked up, but there's not much chance of anyone stealing it."

"Hey, it's not a bad car. It's a classic!" Anthony said, indignant.

Sandy glared. "I meant because it wouldn't move on its own. Don't take an attitude with me, kid. I'm trying to help you."

All the fight drained out of Anthony. "Thank you," he whispered, unable to make his voice any louder. He wanted to be strong and not let them see all his weaknesses, but it was just too much. Instead, he sat on a stack of Budweiser cases and put his head in his hands.

"Okay, Pattyboy. I'll see you and Princess this weekend for dinner, right?"

"Don't call her that, but yeah, we'll be there. We wouldn't miss your summer barbecues."

"Sweet. Well, let me know what's going on later."

The bell above the door jingled, and Anthony watched Sandy walk past the front window, giving a wave as she headed back to her truck. The sun reflected off the steel bars in her ears and through her eyebrow. Anthony had always wanted piercings like that, but he couldn't do them until he turned eighteen. His mother refused to let him get even one. Just another way she didn't understand him.

Focus.

He could feel Patrick's gaze on him but couldn't make himself lift his eyes to meet it. The warmth in those brown eyes made Anthony feel things he didn't want to feel. Chase broke something in him the night of the party, and Jay… well, Jay just took those pieces and ground them into dust. Hope just wasn't something he needed right then.

"I don't know what you're running from," Patrick finally said, "but I can't let you just walk out of here not knowing if you'll be okay. We lost our stocker last week when summer classes started. You can work here to make the money to get your car fixed. I'll pay you nine bucks an hour and give you all the hours I can."

Patrick moved from behind the counter, shuffled past the display on the end, and then leaned against the front. The move was casual, but out of the corner of his eye, Anthony read the tension in the lines of his body. "There's... well, it's not much of an apartment, but there's that storage area above the store I mentioned. You can sleep there and be safe. I got one of those inflatable mattresses we used to use when we went camping. I think it's already up there."

Anthony lifted his head, which seemed to weigh a hundred pounds, and stared openly at Patrick. It took him a minute to find his voice through the chaos of words tumbling around in his mind.

"Why?"

"Why, what?"

"Why would you help me? You don't even know me. What do you...? What do you want in return?" A sick expression passed over Patrick's face, and Anthony looked away. The question needed to be asked. No one helped anyone without a reason. He'd learned that lesson more than a few times at parties where dealers traded sex for drugs. Nothing in life came free.

"Look, I don't know what you're used to, but I don't have sex with kids." Patrick voice only shook a little. "You can work here and sleep upstairs. You don't have to pay for it with your body."

"I'm not a kid."

Patrick gave Anthony a long, appraising look. It wasn't anything perverted, just resigned.

"No, you're probably not. But that doesn't mean I want to take advantage of your situation."

"No? I have a tight little ass and a pretty good mouth. Isn't that what guys want?"

That got a reaction of Patrick. "Jesus, Anthony," he spat. "I'm not going to fuck you. I'm straight. I have a girlfriend. Why can't you just take the fucking help? Why does it have to be a fight?"

Patrick pushed away from the counter in disgust, turning toward the office, probably to call the police and get Anthony the fuck out of his life. That's what everyone did with him, just shoved him in the corner when they were done with him.

Patrick grabbed a cash drawer from the office and shoved it into the register with unnecessary force. He didn't even make a move toward the phone. In that moment, Anthony made the only decision he could. He chose to take the offered hand.

"Thank you for helping me."

Patrick regarded him with a closed expression. Then, with a sigh, he came out from behind the counter and held a hand up.

"You want a tour? You can start today if you want. Just remember that I can't let you behind the counter. You can't sell anything because you're too young to get a license. Or you can get settled upstairs and start tomorrow."

"No, I'll start now." It's not like he had anywhere else to be. His brain spun at the rapid turn of events. Just two nights ago, he was on his knees blowing Chase at a party and trying not to think about the way his life had swirled the drain. Now, he had a place to live and a job at the mercy of a stranger, and Jay, the one who'd said he'd always be there, had disappeared.

With remorse that surprised him, he wondered if Allen knew he'd stolen from their parents yet. He wondered if his brother hated him. It had always been just the two of them, and Anthony had destroyed that in a profound fit of selfishness. Well, except Allen had destroyed it first by abandoning him in favor of Purdue.

Anthony dropped his backpack behind the counter and followed Patrick toward the sales floor.

ANTHONY

"Okay, this first aisle is the big bottles of hard stuff." Patrick pointed as he talked. "On the left, there's whiskey, rum, and vodka. On the right there's tequila, scotch, and everything else. The little bottles like pints, half-pints, and minis are behind the counter. The next aisle is the mixers and premade stuff. After that, we have wine, and then on the floor over there is the beer and such. We keep some cold, but most of the cases are there to stock the coolers. What you're going to do"—he turned his attention to Anthony—"is keep the shelves stocked when you see open spaces, keep the coolers stocked from the beer on the floor, and keep the stuff behind the counter stocked.

"Now." Patrick waved Anthony back behind the aisles to the same hallway between the coolers he'd taken to go to the bathroom. "Back here are the doors to the coolers. The back shelves should also stay stocked so we have enough cold booze for our customers. Any questions so far?"

"No, it's pretty easy to follow." Anthony shivered in the giant walk-in cooler. He made sure there were handles on both sides. The last thing he wanted was to get trapped in there and freeze to death.

He watched Patrick move through the cooler with careful ease. His blue eyes were darker in the dimness, but his cropped, blond hair picked up even the stray ambient light from the giant glass-fronted refrigerator. Anthony could only guess at his age. Thirty, maybe. He had a good build, maybe a little soft, but strong arms and a broad chest.

"Good. Okay, now back here...." Patrick walked out and moved farther into the back rooms. "This is where we store the stock that doesn't fit on the floor. Most of the beer stays out front, but the bottles are in the back, and this little room is where we keep the overstock of pints and half-pints."

Patrick led him into a small room, no larger than an alcove, next to the bathroom. It held small bottles, smaller bottles, and teeny-tiny bottles.

"You've already found the bathroom," Patrick said and then ushered him to another large room farther back. "This is where we keep the overstock of wine."

Anthony nodded. "Okay, that's easy enough."

"Sweet." Patrick grinned. "Let's go back up and do your paperwork, and then you can clock in and get started."

FOR THE NEXT EIGHT hours, Anthony played dumb as he worked the aisles of booze. Deep in his gut, he knew it would be a bad idea to tip his hand about his alcoholic education. Not many seventeen-year-old guys knew the differences in vodkas, whiskeys, and rums quite like Anthony. He'd grown up on them. Instead, he asked inane questions and eventually got most of the store stocked. Around five, a guy came in through the front door and walked right behind the counter like he owned the place.

"Hey, Kevin, I want you to meet our new stocker." Patrick motioned for Anthony to join them at the counter, so he set down the case of Jack he'd been putting on the shelf and shuffled over. "This is Anthony."

"Are you hiring them right out of high school now?" Kevin asked, without so much as a hello to Anthony. The guy was older, older than Anthony or even Patrick, with a potbelly and receding hairline above limp, brown hair. His faded Lions T-shirt gave him the appearance of a jock in decline. He probably had a potbellied wife and two potbellied kids at home next to a refrigerator full of potbellied beer. They'd all sit around eating nachos and listening to daddy swearing at the television whenever his team lost a point. A real all-American, first-world-problem family.

"He was looking for a job, and we need a stocker," Patrick growled. "Besides, I'm pretty sure it's my dad's name on the front of this store, not yours. What do you think?"

Anthony's insides warmed at the man's defense of him. It had been a long time since someone other than Allen defended him against anything.

"Whatever you say, boss. Will Junior be working the night shift, or is that past his bedtime?"

Anthony's face heated, and he looked away, the huge windows at the front drawing his attention.

"He'll be working days with me."

"Whatever pops your cork."

"Come on, Anthony. I'll show you the apartment upstairs." Patrick forestalled whatever Kevin wanted to say with a look so angry, Anthony never wanted it directed at him.

He followed Patrick back through the store to the far end of the pint-and-half-pint room, where they found a door Anthony had missed on their tour. Patrick pulled out two sets of keys, removed a single key from one of them, and handed it to Anthony.

"I'm the only person with the other key to this apartment, so you don't have to worry about the other guys. Okay?"

Anthony nodded and followed Patrick through the unlocked door and up a flight of dank but sturdy stairs. The only light came from the room below, casting monstrous shadows in their path. When they got to the top of their climb, Patrick used the matching key to open the door at and stepped through.

They entered into a stripped and unlived-in kitchen. Gaping holes of missing appliances cut between the dusty countertops. The floor sported myriad discolorations from sunlight and age. Anthony followed Patrick through to the main part of the large room, which was lined with dusty boxes, stacked precariously against walls that were cracked and peeling with neglect.

"The bathroom is through there." Patrick pointed vaguely to the right, and Anthony peeked in to see an old, stained tub, toilet, and sink. Then Patrick walked over to a pile of boxes that looked no different than the rest. It took several tries, opening different ones at random, but he found the one he wanted. Anthony stepped forward and held the box as Patrick wrestled the inflatable mattress from inside it. He laid it on the ground, plugged in the pump, and started the process while Anthony watched.

"I don't have any sheets, but there's a couple of sleeping bags in those same boxes." Patrick nodded toward them. "I think there may be some camp towels in there too. There's no washer and dryer, but I've seen a Laundromat down on either Maywood or Sylvan, I don't remember which."

"Okay."

"There's also a bunch of restaurants up and down the street here and a convenience store across Woodward in the gas station." Patrick didn't seem to be in a rush to get home. He just stood there watching as Anthony took in the offered information. Every so often, he'd run a light hand over his own stomach, as if brushing some imaginary thing from his shirt.

"I'll be okay. You've given me a place to stay. That's more than I could have asked for."

"You have money? I can give you a little—"

"No, I have enough to get me through until we get paid that first time. I'll be careful." Anthony smiled at him, the first true smile since he'd first seen the rundown warehouse-like bookstore where he should have met Jay the night before.

Patrick gave him a small smile in return. "Okay. I'll see you tomorrow... around eight. Wear something dingy. We'll stop by the shop and get the stuff out of your car, and then I'm going to make you clean."

ANTHONY

"I'll be there," Anthony promised. Tension escalated in his chest as Patrick walked back through the door, leaving him alone in the tiny space. His life hadn't stopped spinning since he'd left Chase's car. It was like climbing up an eighty-foot drop just to find an all-day roller coaster over the crest. Now that he'd gotten off the ride, he wasn't sure his legs would hold him up.

He pushed a few boxes out of the way and dropped onto a musty padded chair he found under a pile of dated magazines. Every part of him wanted to crawl onto that air mattress, pull his jacket over his head, and block out the world. But he'd become an adult in the last twenty-four hours whether he'd wanted to or not. He needed to eat, and he needed a plan.

Anthony set his backpack on the mattress and did the slap and tickle of his jeans to make sure he had everything. When his front pockets came up empty, his adrenaline spiked for a second before he realized he'd left his cell phone sitting at home next to the note he'd left his mother, and Sandy the mechanic had his keys. He dumped out the backpack and shoved the laptop and charger back in, stowing a sudden wave of sadness as he headed for the door.

There were no customers in the aisles when Anthony shambled between shelves of wine and made his way up to the counter. No one stood there either. He meandered through an eerie kind of quiet, broken only by the oldies station whispering in the background. Finally, he found Kevin in the front of the beer floor, stacking cases onto a dolly.

"Hey, kid," he said, piling one last case of Miller Genuine Draft on top of the stack already higher than the dolly handle.

"Hi. Do you need some help?" Anthony asked, his voice not much louder than the music playing through the speakers overhead. He didn't want the guy to hate him any more than he already did.

"Nah, I'm just bored and making up six-packs."

"I'm going to get some food. I'll be back in a bit."

Kevin gave him a curt nod, and Anthony took that as an end to the conversation. He'd taken two steps toward the door and just started to wonder which direction he should head when Kevin spoke again.

"Patrick told me about your situation."

He wasn't sure how to respond to that. *Okay? So? And?* He settled on his first choice.

"Okay."

A few long, tense minutes passed. Kevin didn't move from where he stood next to the dolly and Anthony didn't get closer to the door. The song changed on the overhead system. An ambulance rushed up Woodward Avenue. Still, they said nothing.

Finally, an older woman came in through the door, and the beeping sound broke through their little awkward fest. She pulled her purse higher on her flowered shoulder and looked between them for a moment.

"I'm looking for some rum."

That seemed to break Kevin out of his silence.

"Yes, ma'am, how much did you need?"

"Well, the recipe calls for three-quarters of a cup, but I don't know if I can get that little."

Kevin pulled out his phone and typed something into it.

"Okay, it looks like that's just under 200 milliliters, so a half-pint will do it. If it were a cup, you'd need a pint. You don't really need the good stuff either." He righted the dolly and sauntered over behind the counter. Rifling through the small bottles on the shelf, Kevin grabbed one and held it out to the woman. She pushed a stray hair back into her coif before taking it.

Anthony's stomach snarled like something was trying to escape, and he headed for the door, leaving Kevin to deal with the woman.

"Hey, there's a pizza place if you go a block to your left," Kevin called after him. "It's cheap and the food is good."

"Uhm, thanks. You want anything?"

"Nah, I brought something, but thanks."

Anthony turned left once he went out the door. The quiet street stretched out before him with miles of open sidewalk. He glanced around and saw he was just a short walk from the highway. It seemed like forever since his car limped off I-696 and his life crash-landed right in front of Patrick's store. It felt like going forward instead of backward as he wandered up Woodward toward the promise of pizza and maybe a new life.

Trees littered the roadside, casting evening shadows across the sidewalk. It didn't look much different than the business districts near his house back in DeKalb. As he followed the cracks in the cement, Anthony tried to memorize his surroundings. Twelve hundred dollars would take him forever to save up, maybe even the entire summer. He'd be there for a while. Besides, he couldn't call for help if he got lost and couldn't find Mears Liquors again.

The tiny pizza place sat on the quiet side of a four-way intersection just two blocks from the liquor store. It took almost no time at all for him to pull the door open and stand, wide-eyed, before the huge overhead menu. The unfed beast in his stomach roared at the selection: sandwiches and Stromboli, salads and pizza, every possible combination of foods he loved.

A meatball sandwich sounded good, so he ordered one with fries, smiling at the teenage girl who tried to flirt as she took his money. He had less than no interest in flirting back, and not just because he wasn't into girls, but because it was all he could do to hold on to his merry-go-round of a life. It had all happened in a daze, as if nothing had become real yet. He'd wake up tomorrow in his dank little basement room, ready for another party with Chase and fighting with his mother instead of being a homeless, friendless thief trapped by his own misfortune.

Loneliness settled over Anthony as he took the bag from the cashier and shuffled over to one of the small booths that lined the front window. Even after what had happened, he missed Chase so much it hurt. Chase had been there when Allen deserted him for college. He had no one now. Not even Jay, who'd promised Anthony he'd never hurt him.

Carlos_Pizza came up in the list of available open Wi-Fi networks when he powered up his laptop. Anthony checked his email first. Nothing from Jay. He didn't even get a note to ask if he had a place to stay or if he was okay. The sting radiated in his chest with an empty ache he couldn't quit describe. He had an email from Allen from earlier that day, so he opened it.

Where the fuck are you? If you don't want to stay with mom and dad, come down here. You can stay with me. Hell, you can go to school down here if you want. Melanie is fine with you staying with us. Call me and let me know you're okay.

So Allen had finally figured out Anthony still existed. He hadn't heard from his brother in so long, except for the occasional Facebook comment. Anthony couldn't even remember the last meaningful conversation they'd had. He didn't reply. It wouldn't be too long before they noticed the missing money, and Allen wouldn't be so accommodating with a place to stay then. They'd label Anthony a thief, and no one wanted one of those staying in their house.

He didn't log into his Facebook page because his posts usually had a label of where he was, so obviously Facebook would know. Instead, he just went to his profile as a visitor. There were no new posts on his profile. No one even noticed he was gone. He switched over to Chase's profile and found a wall full of real-time pictures from the graduation ceremony that started about an hour before. No one mentioned the fact they were missing one of the graduates. There were smiles all around, and none bigger than Chase's.

Tears burned in the back of Anthony's throat as he slammed the laptop closed.

The door tone sounded when he went back into the liquor store. Kevin sat behind the counter, mechanically putting together six-packs of beer from the cases. He ripped another six-pack holder from the roll and popped in the first can.

"The old lady was a lush. Recipe my ass. She traded in the half-pint for a fifth after you left. Unless she's got a bake sale going on for all of Detroit, she's gonna be juiced up by the time *Wheel of Fortune* comes on."

Anthony snorted and headed for the stairs.

A SOUND RIPPED HIM from the first solid sleep he'd had in days, and Anthony bolted upright on the mattress, his gaze flying around to the dark corners of an unfamiliar room. He heard it again, a muffled thump. It took almost a minute before he figured out where he was. His basement home remained far away. Instead, he now stayed in the apartment above the store. The sounds below him in the dead of night could only mean someone had broken in. With no cell phone and no phone in the apartment, he couldn't even call for help.

What if they find the staircase leading to the apartment?

He'd locked the door. He would be safe. But he couldn't just let someone ransack the store, not after everything Patrick had done for him.

He slid back into his jeans and tennis shoes and crept to the door. No other sound made its way from the first floor. Maybe they'd gone. He should definitely go down now and call Patrick from the office phone. Patrick had written his number on top of the employee phone list Anthony had seen in the office on his tour.

The door creaked open with only a wisp of sound, thank God. Anthony crept down the stairs, his shoes making no noise, and he let out a breath on each piece of wood. If anyone remained, Anthony didn't want to give him or her any warning he approached. Only one stair creaked as he put weight on it. Anthony didn't so much as breathe as he moved to the next step. His hand trembled on the railing.

Anthony knew exactly the kind of damage human beings could inflict on one another, and he didn't want to end up like Aaron.

The door at the bottom of the staircase swung open with as little noise as the one at the top. He snuck toward the opening of the pint room and wondered if the intruders could hear his heart pounding as loudly as he could. Movement reflected in the glass bottles just outside the mouth of the back room, and Anthony froze. Low, harsh panting followed, and he took a step forward and then another. It sounded as if someone were hurt. He wished it had occurred to him to find some kind of weapon before he came down. Instead, he pulled a fifth of Stoli from one of the open cases at his feet and peeked around the corner of the cooler.

He damned near dropped the bottle.

"Fuck," a quiet voice moaned. Anthony stared openmouthed at the couple doing just that across a stack of beer cases. He nearly stormed from his hiding place and demanded to know what right they thought they had to fuck in Patrick's store—but then he recognized the closely cropped hair of the man buried inside the woman holding on to the cases.

"Harder, Patrick," she moaned. Patrick leaned down, and she turned her upper body just enough to catch his mouth in an animalistic kiss. The woman's long, brown hair curtained her face as she held on to the case to keep Patrick from pushing her to the ground with his enthusiastic thrusts.

"Feel good, babe?" Patrick asked, his words a little slurred, and he took a tighter hold on her pale ass.

"God, yeah. You should pull out and jizz all over the cases. Sell them to unsuspecting drunks with your spooge on the label."

Patrick laughed, an insubstantial, breathy sound before he pushed the woman down over the cases and started to move again. Anthony's feet couldn't quite move, and even though he'd never been into chicks, his cock pushed insistently against the fly of his jeans. The way they kissed as they fucked, the way Patrick buried his face in the woman's hair, it opened something in Anthony's soul, a longing he wasn't sure had ever existed before.

Sure, he wanted to fuck like that. What guy didn't? But the connection they seemed to share—the need and want and affection—those things made Anthony feel incredibly alone as he watched.

As if he'd heard Anthony's thoughts, Patrick reached up and entwined his fingers with the woman's where they gripped the top case. The contrast between Patrick's strong, masculine fingers and the woman's soft, delicate ones stuck with Anthony as the couple raced toward their inevitable conclusions. He'd wanted that with Chase, so fucking badly. He didn't need cuddly mani-pedi time or anything. Just some measure of affection.

Anthony didn't stick around for the drunken, sticky aftermath. He couldn't. First, he didn't want to see their post-sex kissing and touching, but more pressing was the ache in his dick. He turned, careful not to let his shoes make any noise on the dingy floor, and crept back up the stairs to his inflatable bed.

The predawn air chilled Anthony when he kicked off his shoes and dropped his jeans around the erection tenting them. He crawled between the two sleeping bags he'd spread over the mattress and tried to ignore the throbbing between his legs. Pressing the heel of his hand against the base just made it worse.

The image of a nameless, faceless guy bending him over that case shot a thrill through Anthony, and he couldn't stop himself from jerking the briefs off his cock and down the tops of his thighs. He hadn't so much as thought about sex since the humiliating incident on his knees at the party. For now, he pushed that to the back of his mind and focused on the idea of that boy touching him. He didn't want it to be Chase or Jay or anyone else who would make him feel unwanted. Right then, he wanted to be wanted.

He snaked a hand down his torso and wrapped trembling fingers around his dick. Tense and hot and hard, he ached with the need to jack off. He imagined himself bent over that same stack, gripping the sides for dear life as someone slammed into him from behind. His muscles flexed and his eyes closed as he pulled Anthony back onto his dick.

Anthony could almost feel the stretch he'd never experienced.

When he'd jacked off before, he'd always imagined himself fucking another guy, but the wild need in that woman's voice made Anthony wonder what it would be like to be fucked. He hesitated before sliding two fingers into his mouth, from his left hand so the right could keep stroking. Sweat beaded his forehead, and Anthony tried not to think about anything other than the feeling of his hands on his body. And then, as he slid those two spit-slick fingers into his ass, the feeling of them *in* his body.

He moaned into the darkness, his body arching, spreading his legs wider. The stretch scared him, as though maybe he was doing something wrong. Then, the pop of penetration opened his body, and he groaned. It felt better than he'd thought it would. He pulled a knee toward his chest to get better access to his ass, and the sensitive underside of his balls rubbed against the skin on top of his hand. God, that just made it better.

ANTHONY

The sounds coming from his throat swelled into quiet cries as he rode his fingers and concentrated his other hand on the head of his cock in short, spastic strokes. It wouldn't take long, not while he imagined a guy's low grunts or the way he would beg to be fucked harder. Anthony's head fell back against the pillow as another scissoring flash of discomfort made his dick pulse. He jerked his hips up, fucking his hand. So close, he was so close. His cock throbbed as he tightened his grip and forced his fingers deeper.

Do you like that? The quiet idea of a stranger's voice in the back of his mind made his balls tighten, and he closed his eyes tight against the white-hot flash that began his orgasm. All of the pent-up anxiety, all of the confusion and pain, rushed out of him in a blinding splatter of come across his stomach. His silent, openmouthed cry lasted until he trembled with the power of his release. Then, slowly, he let his fingers slide from his body and brought a come-slicked hand up to cover his eyes with his forearm.

Anthony forced harsh breaths out and took deeper ones in, trying to calm himself. Jesus, he couldn't believe he'd just jacked off because he'd seen his boss fucking his girlfriend on the sales floor. That was about ten different kinds of wrong. His ass still tingled from the rough, blunt thrust of his fingers, and his cock sang with release.

Anthony delayed crawling off the inflatable mattress to clean up. He lay there as long as he could, sticky and exhausted, while he tried to figure out how he could face Patrick the next day.

Chapter Six

Patrick ran through the drive-thru and got a couple of artery-clogging muffins, some hash browns, some coffee for him, and a Coke for Anthony. Patrick was surprised he hadn't even considered not picking up food for the boy. He didn't need another weight hanging around his neck—the store and his brother were more than enough. Hell, even Danielle had started becoming irritatingly clingy, just what he didn't need.

A knot formed between his shoulder blades, tensing up his spine as he left the drive-thru and aimed the RAV4 back toward the store. The same routine, over and over: the store, his brother, a bit of sex, and then his life started all over again. It would continue that way until something gave.

He'd been at it for two years. Something *had* to give.

Relief flooded Patrick when he tried the front doors only to find them locked. At least he'd been sober enough to do that last night after he'd finished screwing Danielle's brains out in the middle of the sales floor. He'd met Danielle over at One-Eyed Betty's about a year before. It started out as nothing, a couple of single people looking for a fuck, but then the sex became regular and they fell into a routine—which is exactly what you want from sex, right, a routine?

He balanced the drink carrier on his leg and pulled his keys from his left hand, which held their breakfast. After a little finesse, a little juggling, and a bit of Coke wetting the thigh of his jeans, Patrick got through the door and set the food on the counter. He shooed away the dirty-looking man trying to come in behind him for a morning buzz. Christ, he didn't know what was worse—the fear he'd walk into a gun one night, or watching people destroying themselves on the shit he sold.

Only the hum of the coolers greeted Patrick as he glanced around the store. For a heart-stopping moment, he wondered if Anthony had fled. Then he remembered he'd unlocked the doors when he came in. The kid had no way of relocking them if he left. It seemed ominous he hadn't come downstairs yet, though. Even a teenager couldn't sleep like the dead on an inflatable mattress, in a strange room, with so many questions hanging over his head.

Patrick grabbed the grease-stained bag, balanced it on top of the drinks, and headed for the pint room with the staircase that led to the apartment. The place had never had any kind of tenant, though Bren often talked about moving up there *Before*. That Before had a big ol' capital *B* on it—before a junkie with a gun fucked up their lives. Before his brother was unable to leave the house. Before Patrick became the rock everyone in his life needed for stability.

Before.

At the top of the stairs, he paused. It seemed stupid to knock on his own door, but he couldn't force himself to walk in. Patrick wanted Anthony to feel safe. More than anything, he wanted the kid to feel as though he had options and space. Bren hadn't felt like that since the shooting, and it fucked him up. So he tapped on the door. It took almost a full minute, but eventually, the door opened, and sadness sucker-punched Patrick right in the gut. Anthony's eyes were red and swollen, his face pale, and his shoulders hunched, as if the weight of the world rested there.

ANTHONY

"Hey, I brought breakfast. Are you okay?"

Tears slid from the corners of Anthony's tired, frightened eyes. He didn't even bother to wipe them away. He simply took a step back to let Patrick in the door. Patrick took that as a welcome and stepped into the living area. He set the food and drinks on the only chair with nothing in it and then moved boxes off a small table and the other chair. Anthony stood by the door as if he hadn't noticed. It took a minute for the boy to take those few steps into the room with him, both physically and, it seemed, mentally.

Patrick laid out the contents of the bag, balancing the hash browns on top of napkins so they wouldn't touch the dusty table. He pulled the drinks from the carrier and set them out. By the time he'd laid everything out, Anthony stood next to his chair.

"Hey, I know things seem bad right now, but they're going to get better." Patrick reached out, paused, and then let his hand rub the outside of Anthony's arm.

Anthony turned his gaze to the window near his makeshift bed.

"I found an open Wi-Fi signal from one of your neighbors." Anthony's gaze never left the window. Patrick wondered if it were easier for him to talk to it than to Patrick.

"I'll give you the store's password. You can use it," he told Anthony, his voice almost a whisper, unwilling to break the tenuous grip the boy seemed to have on himself.

"I checked my email and there wasn't anything from Jay. There was nothing from Chase. Nothing from my parents. I checked their Facebook pages and only Chase posted anything about me leaving." He shook his head, and the pain in his expression brought a lump to Patrick's throat.

"What did it say?"

"It said, 'I'm glad he's gone. Hashtag-Downer.' That's what he always called me, 'Downer.' And nothing on my page, or anyone else's page. I just checked again and there's still nothing. They don't even care that I'm gone."

Anger welled inside Patrick. "You said you left your phone so they can't text or call. They didn't send you any messages on Facebook or anything?" Even when he'd lived in Ohio for school and then after, he still kept up with the people in his life, especially his dad and brother. What kind of family cut off their kid like that? No wonder Anthony left.

"I didn't log in," Anthony admitted. "I don't know all the settings and didn't want to take the chance that they could use it to find me. That's how they found Aaron."

"Who's Aaron?"

"Aaron's my older brother. He... he got kidnapped when he was younger, and I don't know exactly how, but I guess they traced the GPS on his phone and found him. Not in time, though."

"I'm so sorry, Anthony."

"He's not dead. He just wishes he was."

Just like Bren.

He couldn't stand the pain in Anthony's eyes, so he kicked the chair out and asked the boy to sit down.

"We have a lot to do today, Anthony. You need to eat." Patrick paused for a long moment before adding, "Please."

Anthony sat down and reached for the sandwich, now almost cold in its greasy paper wrapping. Patrick opened his too because he couldn't think of anything to do to erase the pain in the kid's face. God, if this was what having kids felt like, he was glad he'd stayed single and childless.

"What do we have to do today, Ferb?"

"What?"

ANTHONY

"Never mind." A smirk ghosted around the corners of Anthony's mouth.

Patrick let it go. "Well, we're getting in a shipment of liquor, and it has to be checked and put away. I also want to show you some other things about the store." He unwrapped his sandwich. "I forgot to tell you last night that there are security cameras in most areas of the store, and we have a motion-activated alarm. So, once you come up here, you need to stay up here, or you'll set off the alarms and the police will come. I hate to make you a prisoner, but at least for now, can you do that for me?" Patrick took the first bite of his cold sandwich. The eggs congealed in his mouth, and he quickly sipped his lukewarm coffee.

"Great, I traded a basement for an attic." Anthony flicked the straw in his soda. "Well, at least it's got a better view."

"I don't even know you," Patrick pointed out. "I can't trust you with keys to my store yet. What do you want from me?"

Anthony shrugged, a halfhearted, spastic thing as he took another drink of soda. He didn't seem to have any other hostile comments.

"Are we still good? You still want to stay?"

The kid ignored Patrick's question and said instead, "Kevin told me about the cameras last night when I went out for food. I won't come down... well, unless I hear something."

Patrick searched Anthony's face, but the boy just kept eating. Had he heard them fucking last night? Had he come down? He'd had a few beers before Danielle showed up and they decided to christen the beer with their own personal happy juice. Anthony's expression didn't change when he reached for his Coke, so Patrick decided to let it go. He wouldn't be having sex in the store again anyway. He was already going to catch hell from Bren.

Then what Anthony said really started to sink in.

"No fucking way." Patrick kept his voice firm, allowing no room for argument. "If you hear anything, you keep your ass upstairs. In fact, when you come up, take the cordless with you so you can call the police if anything happens. The doors lock from the inside with a manual lock, so you can get out if you need to." He leaned forward and caught Anthony's wide-eyed gaze. "There is *nothing*, and I mean *nothing* in this store worth your life. Do you understand me?"

His heart pounded as he tried to get his meaning through to Anthony. There'd been enough carnage in that store. Something in him ached at the thought of Anthony hurt or even killed by an intruder. God, he'd left the cameras off last night, left the store without setting the alarm. Some big badass protector he was.

"Okay, Jesus." Anthony sat frozen, the straw halfway to his mouth.

"I'm not kidding, Anthony. You call the fucking police."

"*Okay.*" Anthony rolled his eyes.

It was less than Patrick wanted but probably all he'd get.

Then, under Anthony's breath, he heard, "God. Good thing you didn't get the strokerritto."

Patrick blew out a sigh and ignored it.

"I'm usually here every morning by eight a.m. After you've been here for a while, let's say a thirty-day probation, I'll give you the codes and a key."

"You don't have to do that. I can stay up here until eight."

"I know, but I don't want you to feel like a prisoner here."

"I'm less of a prisoner here than I was at home."

Patrick couldn't decide which broke his heart more—the words or the matter-of-fact way Anthony said them.

"Would you mind doing me a favor today?" he asked.

"It's not like you're giving me a place to stay or anything. What kind of favor?"

ANTHONY

"Some guys are coming to fix the air-conditioning at my parents' house. My brother... well... he doesn't leave the house. If they need him to go outside and look at something, he can't."

"You mean he's agoraphobic?"

Patrick shook his head. "*Stubborn* is more the word I'd use. Would you mind staying at the house for a bit and talking to the guys? If you have questions, you can use Bren's phone to call and ask me."

"Sure. Is it okay if I bring a book?"

"You probably should anyway. My brother isn't much of a conversationalist."

They finished their breakfast in silence, and Patrick waited while Anthony threw on shoes before they headed together for the store downstairs. He didn't try to break the boy's mood but simply let him work in peace and watched out of the corner of his eye as Anthony folded in on himself. If he could get that kid's mother in a room for five minutes, he'd give her some serious lessons on parenting. Something else had happened with that Chase kid, and he was sure Anthony would tell him in time. But the other one, Jay, he just couldn't figure out. Why get the kid to drive all the way up here from Chicago just to meet him in a bookstore parking lot? Worse, why blow him off because he missed the meeting by a day? If the kid really did want Anthony to stay with him, why not just give out his home address? The questions frustrated Patrick to the point that he didn't want to think about them anymore. It wasn't his business anyway.

"Patrick?"

He looked up to see Anthony watching him from near the front coolers.

"Yeah, kid?"

"How many hours did you want me to work each week?"

Shit, he hadn't even thought about it.

"I don't know. Let me grab the schedule and work something out for this week."

He stepped into the small office behind the counter and grabbed that week's schedule from the pegboard next to the time clock. Realistically, he needed Anthony for about twenty hours a week, but he couldn't get the boy's haunted expression out of his head, so he worked in an extra day. The store did okay business, not enough to warrant the extra time, but he'd justify it to himself and Bren later.

"I can only go up to twenty-nine hours. By law, if you work thirty hours or more, I have to give you health insurance, and neither of us can afford that. I filled you in on the schedule, working days with me, mostly."

He handed Anthony a piece of paper with his new schedule. The kid studied it for a long time and then shoved it in his pocket.

"I can do that."

Chapter Seven

"Bren, come on, man, open the door."

The muffled sound of his brother's voice bored into Bren's head as he rumbled to consciousness against the musty couch cushions. Sunlight streamed in between the curtains he'd left wide open to the street for anyone who cared to see him passed out in the living room. The brightness scored his brain like a drill bit from hell, sharp and harsh, ripping his head open from the inside. He couldn't tell if the pounding came from the door or the throbbing of his temples.

"Dude, you know I have a key," Patrick yelled, slamming something into the bottom of the door. The wood held, but Bren didn't want to risk having to replace the damn door, so he rolled off the couch and onto the floor.

"Fuck," Bren murmured to no one as his elbow slammed into the coffee table. It took a minute for him to find his feet, and he hoisted himself up with significant help from the surrounding furniture. Shivering, he shuffled toward the door Patrick had just tried to take off the hinges despite his reminder of a key. It took a minute and a few more feet closer to the door for Bren to realize he heard more than one voice.

He turned the dead bolt, pulled hard on the knob, and staggered back as the door flew open to admit his brother and some teenage boy. His brain kicked in and he recognized the kid from the video. Right. Goddamn it. Not only did he have to deal with Patrick and a hangover, but he had to deal with a stranger too. What the fuck was Patrick thinking? He took consolation from the fact his brother looked like shit too, his eyes bloodshot and his face rough and unshaven.

Patrick stepped inside, the kid close behind, and Bren closed the door, trying to ignore the beer bottles littering every surface. Some of them were turned on their sides, staining the carpet with his indifference.

"Jesus, man, it's ten o'clock in the fucking morning. How are you still wasted?" Patrick stormed past him and into the kitchen. He didn't need to help his brother find anything because Bren hadn't moved so much as a chair since their father died. Patrick rooted around in the cabinet, and then Bren heard the pop of air into a garbage bag being flicked open.

"Mom would be appalled; you know that, right?" The pity in Patrick's voice warred with the look of disgust on his face. All the while, the kid just stood against the wall, soaking up Bren's humiliation. At least he didn't have puke on his shirt. That would have iced the cake nicely. He dropped onto the couch and put his head in his hands. Twenty-six years old and he still needed a fucking babysitter.

"Yeah, well, Mom ain't here. Neither of them are here. I'm here. The world got screwed in *that* trade." Bren let Patrick continue cleaning while the boy said nothing and watched them both.

He couldn't go on like this.

It was gonna fucking kill him.

Except for the litter of booze and takeout containers, time could have stopped in the house and no one would have known. Nothing had changed. The same pictures still peppered the bookcase, showing a chronology of their lives. Dust choked the plastic flowers his mother had put in a vase on the table next to the aging couch, a testament to the fact their father'd never had the heart to change anything, either.

He glanced at the pictures and saw the stark contrast to the guy he used to be. He had the same dark brown hair as their father, the same brown eyes, though his were now rimmed with a permanent red glaze. Alcohol and stress had stripped thirty pounds from his already thin frame, leaving him gaunt and sickly. Another bottle clattered in the bag as he turned back to Patrick.

"How do you even get this shit?" Patrick asked him, picking up another bottle. The kid had shifted into motion by then, grabbing two-day-old Chinese takeout containers from the floor-table area and shoving them in the bag Patrick still held.

"The grocery service doesn't just deliver food."

"Are you *kidding* me? You *buy* beer when you own a fucking liquor store?"

"Are you going to bring it to me?"

Patrick threw the last bottle into the bag on top of a pizza box that appeared to be older than the kid who handed it to him.

"You haven't tried going back to the store in almost a year. We could—"

"The store that had all the cameras off last night?"

"Oh shit, Bren, I—"

"Why did you turn off the fucking cameras?"

Patrick sighed again. His brother seemed to be doing a lot of that lately where Bren was concerned.

"Because you didn't need to watch us fucking."

Bren huffed, blowing off the concern as if his brother plowing his girlfriend on camera didn't matter.

"I couldn't see you."

"I know. I turned off the one thing you needed so I could feel human for a few minutes," Patrick shot back, and his expression appeared almost as pained as Bren's felt.

"I couldn't see you," he repeated. "You were in that fucking store, and I couldn't see if you were safe. I have to know. I have to call... police... keep.... Can't... I can't...."

"Bren, take a breath. It's okay. Shhhhh...." Patrick stood next to the couch and rubbed his brother's back for a minute. "I'm going to get your pills."

Before Bren could object, Patrick jogged into the bathroom. It had been their parents' bathroom at one time, but now the house belonged to Bren. He didn't want it, but he couldn't force himself to do anything else with it. It took a minute, and Bren could hear him going through all the bottles of medications Bren refused to take, but eventually he found something. He had a bottle in one hand and a small cup of water when he returned. He shook out a pill one-handed—and then he slammed both cup and bottle onto the table with a force that would have shattered them if they'd been glass.

"God damn it, Bren." He dropped the pill back in the bottle. Frustration tightened his entire frame, and Bren looked away. Patrick fell back onto the couch and rubbed Bren's back again.

"You can't take the Xanax while you're drinking. They won't mix. Let's just sit here for a while, okay?"

"I can't keep you safe if I can't see you," Bren whispered. "Not there. Not in that place. You can't turn off the cameras. Don't you have a bed in your townhouse? Can't you fuck there?"

"Okay, I'm sorry. I wasn't thinking."

"Speaking of not thinking, why did you let that kid stay? You don't know anything about him. He's a total stranger, Patrick. Dad would have—"

"Dad would have helped him, Bren."

Bren couldn't argue with that. It was the truth.

"He's seventeen and was about to be living in his car. We were without a stocker. It made sense. No one is using the apartment above the store. I set up one of those inflatable mattresses we used to use when we went camping. It's not like he has keys, and the alarms are on downstairs."

"You really think it's safe to let him stay?" Bren asked.

"Yeah, I do. He's a scared kid."

"You do realize I'm standing right here, right?" the kid asked, annoyed.

Bren lifted his head to glare at him. "Scared kids do stupid things."

They looked at each other for a long time before Patrick answered.

"Maybe if someone had helped Carter Ford, he wouldn't have come to the store that day with a gun."

Bren recoiled at the harsh sound of the name. They didn't say it often. In fact, Bren never said it at all. He didn't want to talk about the man who had destroyed their lives, didn't want to think about him.

"Just be careful, Patrick, please. You're all I have left."

Patrick wrapped his arms around his brother, holding on for all he had.

"Still here...," the kid said, but Bren's head jerked up toward Patrick.

"You *did* set the alarm when you and Princess left last night, right?"

"I... I think so."

Bren recognized the lie and gave him a disgusted look. He pushed away from Patrick and got up to cross to a computer that was set up on the old table they and their parents used to eat around growing up. He moved the mouse and the screen lit up, already at the login for the store's security system.

"Don't you ever go anywhere else on this thing?" Patrick asked. "Jesus, Bren, download some porn or something."

The kid snorted at that. Bren had forgotten he was even there.

"Shut up." Bren's cheeks heated as his hands flew over the keyboard, entering the password and bringing up the dashboard for their security system. Patrick never went into the software. If he needed something, like running through the footage to see if the guy with the winter coat in July had stolen anything, or if an employee was pilfering, he let Bren take care of it. It was the only thing he could do to help Patrick with the store.

"No, you didn't set the alarm. God, if you don't want to run the store, just fucking sell it. I don't care anymore."

"Yes, you do."

Bren turned away from Patrick and marched into the bathroom, slamming the door behind him. Before their world changed, Bren would have bantered, always wanting to get the last word. Now he walked away before the fight got out of hand because he couldn't stand to lose the one person left in his life.

"Okay, you win," Patrick called after him. "I won't turn the cameras off again. Just don't be mad at me, Bren. I'm alone enough as it is."

"Whatever," Bren yelled in response to Patrick's admission. He took a deep breath. God, you could hear everything in this house. In fact, some days when Patrick stayed away, he could still hear the ghosts of how their lives used to be. Maybe that's why he refused to step outside the door, because the sounds of ghosts in the house comforted him.

He stood at the sink and splashed cold water on his face, trying to feel human again. Then he grabbed the toothbrush and toothpaste to clear his mouth as well as his head. Finally, after maybe five minutes of alone time, Bren stepped out of the bathroom, seeing his brother's surprised expression before he rubbed a towel over his face. He tossed it back into the bathroom and threw a sharp nod in the kid's direction.

"You gonna introduce me to your little friend?" Bren asked, trying to take the focus off his fucked-up head.

"Wait, you mean I'm still here?" the kid asked.

His brother stalled for just a moment, and it looked as though he wanted to say something else, but instead, Patrick pulled the boy forward and Bren got a good, nonfuzzy look. He was tall and lanky like Bren, but without the alcoholic emaciation. His eyes were a little red, and Bren knew that look all too well. He looked past the artfully torn jeans, the band T-shirt, and even the black-painted fingernails and saw a soul older than he was, maybe even older than Patrick. This kid had lived through something, and it was eating him from the inside out.

"Anthony, this is my brother, Brendan. Bren, this is our new stocker, Anthony." Bren could hear the weariness around the edges of each word from Patrick's mouth.

"Your adopted kid, you mean?"

"Shut—"

"Fuck you, I'm not a kid." Anthony pushed Bren's outstretched hand away. A fire blazed under the surface of his pale skin. Bren wanted to reach out and touch it, see if it burned his skin. Instead, he shrugged off the feeling.

"Whatever, Munchkin. You're the one living in the attic of some guy you don't even know because Mommy and Daddy are mean."

"You don't know anything about me."

"Let me guess, they took away your PlayStation?"

A flush rose on Anthony's cheeks, and Bren wondered if he'd hit a nerve. But instead of backing down, Anthony just leaned forward so their faces were almost touching. He didn't say anything immediately but took a deep breath.

"No, they threw me in the basement and forgot about me for nearly a decade. They sacrificed me to my brother's fucked-up demons. Looks like Patrick may know a little about what that's like."

Bren reeled, the shock of Anthony's words like a hot iron on his already tenuous mood. He understood exactly what that meant, because he was the brother with the altar and Patrick, the sacrifice.

Patrick stared at Anthony, the concussion of his bombshell response sending waves of understanding through the ramshackle living room. Bren could see the resemblances between the boy and Patrick—squared shoulders carrying the weight of the world, eyes that had seen too much and slept too little, and then of course, the wariness, waiting for the meltdown of an unstable brother.

"What kind of demons does your brother have?" Bren asked before he could stop himself. It shouldn't matter. He didn't want to take on anything else. His own demons were enough for anyone, but the anger in Anthony's voice made him pause.

"He watched his best friend being raped and murdered while he suffered the same. The only reason he survived is because the guys fucked up cutting his throat."

Bren didn't even have to glance at Patrick to know what ran through his brother's mind. He'd been exactly right to help this kid. No, he wasn't a kid. He'd grown up soon after his brother's madness had ripped through his life. Much like Bren's madness had ripped through Patrick's life.

"Jesus, I don't even know what to say," Patrick murmured and ran a trembling hand along the front of his shirt. He'd been doing that for as long as Bren could remember. It had gotten worse the day the man with the gun tore their lives apart for some spare change and booze.

"There isn't anything to say," Anthony told them. "That's just the way it is. Aaron had night terrors and flashbacks. For the first few years my parents kept him doped to the gills. They threw me and my other brother into the basement so they could deal with him. He'd freak out about anything and nothing."

"I know that feeling," Bren admitted, and Patrick jerked his head toward Bren.

"You have flashbacks? Like the guys who come back from war, or something?"

"I don't go back and live it again, no. But the memory is there, all the time. The pills and the booze makes it not so hard to see. You weren't there, Patrick. You didn't see the bullet tear him open. You didn't watch him bleed out all over the floor. You didn't see the look in that guy's eyes as he put a bullet in me. You can't understand." Bren hated the pleading note in his own voice.

"I was eight hundred miles away while my father was murdered and my kid brother clung to life," Patrick shot back. "My whole fucking family brutally attacked, and there wasn't a goddamn thing I could do but drive faster. Then I got there, and I just sat by your bed. God, so many times, I wished it were me so I wouldn't have to deal with the funeral, the cops, and the fucking crime scene cleanup. But this?" Patrick waved an arm around the mess in the living room. "This I wouldn't wish on anyone."

"Me either." Bren got tired of hoping his legs would hold and dropped onto the couch, narrowly missing a closed pizza box. He couldn't remember the last time he'd had pizza. Patrick sat on the other end of the coffee table and shoved the box into the already overstuffed garbage bag.

"And look, Bren, I know you hate me for leaving, for not being there, but—"

"No, I don't. I never did. The store wasn't your thing, it was mine. You had your own life. Jesus, I know, I should just let you sell it or close it or whatever, but it just.... It feels like that's all I have left, even if it's not mine."

Anthony pushed away from the wall, forgotten in the chaos of their confessions. He dropped like a pile of bones into an armchair no one ever used. A cloud of dust plumed up around him, and he coughed, breaking the moment.

"Bren—"

"Anyway, want to tell me why you guys stopped by at the ass crack of dawn and woke me up?" He didn't want to talk about it anymore. Talking about it made it all real again, and he didn't want any of it to be real.

"The AC guy is going to be here by two to fix the compressor. I know you don't like dealing with people, and he may need someone to go outside with him. So I'm going to leave Anthony here to help. He can't run the register at the store, so I have to be there."

Patrick stood, inching his way toward the door, and Bren glared up at him.

"You're sending a seventeen-year-old to babysit me now?" Rage still burned his skin.

"Are you going to leave the porch?" Patrick asked not unkindly.

"No."

"Then yes."

"Outstanding. When the preschool lets out, make sure you send someone to watch over him."

"You're kind of a dick," Anthony observed, dropping a battered paperback book onto the coffee table in front of him as he scrounged through a worn orange backpack.

"Well, on that note," Patrick said with wary determination, "I'm going to leave you two to get to know each other. One of you call and let me know how the repairs went and that you didn't murder each other. Anthony, I'll pick you up once the guy leaves. You'll get paid for being here."

"Great, now he's a paid babysitter."

"Good luck, Anthony."

The door closed behind Patrick, and Bren wanted to throw something at it. Fucking Patrick and his fucking babysitter. So he couldn't leave the house. He could open a window and talk to the repair guy through it. He wasn't totally useless.

Well.

Yeah.

He kind of was.

"What are you reading?"

"*Harry Potter and the Deathly Hallows*. It's the last book in the series."

"I've never read them," Bren admitted.

"Maybe you should. It looks like you have some time on your hands here. The series is one of the few things I brought with me. You can borrow them if you want."

"You really are a trusting little thing, aren't you? Don't you know that monsters go bump in the night here?"

"Monsters go bump in the night everywhere. And I don't trust you, but I *do* trust your brother."

"Fair enough. You want a beer?"

"So you can tell Patrick?" Anthony asked.

"No, because I need one and it sounds like maybe you do too. Besides, what else are we gonna do while we wait for the repair guy?" Bren gave Anthony an appraising look.

"Yeah, I'll take a beer."

"Come on, then." Bren hauled himself off the couch and led Anthony into the kitchen. Dishes sat in the sink from God knows when. Cereal bowls, pizza plates, Chinese takeout forks piled on top of each other in a heap. It was as if he had food ADD. If he actually had to mix more than two or three things together to make it into a meal, he wasn't interested. On rare occasions, Bren made grilled cheese and tomato soup because something in his soul needed it. His mother had made it for him growing up, when the kids at school were mean or his big brother had better things to do than hang around with him. Bren thought maybe if he ate enough of it, it would make him feel better like it had then.

There wasn't enough fucking soup in the world for that.

Bren pulled two bottles out of the refrigerator, which contained more beer than food. His half of the life insurance from their father's death left him without money troubles, at least for a while. He hadn't had any debt, and the house was paid off, so he just needed the alcohol to numb his brain and the food to keep his body alive. Patrick took care of everything else.

"Where are you from, k—Anthony?" Bren stopped himself at the memory of rage in Anthony's face when he'd called him a kid.

"Just outside Chicago." Anthony popped the top off the beer like a pro and took a long pull. *Oh, yeah, this kid knows his way around a bottle too.*

"So, of all the places you could have gone, why the hell would you come to Detroit?"

"I thought I had a friend here. Turns out, not so much."

"Yeah, I thought I had a lot of friends here. Turns out fifteen minutes up the road is just too far to go to visit the madman."

"That's what Aaron used to call himself, the madman." Anthony dropped into one of the chairs, and Bren joined him.

"Sometimes, no matter what polite society tries to tell you, it's true." Bren tipped his beer in salute.

"My turn," Anthony announced, and while Bren's shoulders tensed in anticipation, he nodded. Tit for tat.

"Go ahead."

"Why can't you deal with the repair guy?"

"That, my friend, is the question of the year. My brother brought me here when I got out of the hospital because it's the only home I've ever lived in. He told me later that I just kept saying that I wanted to go home. Shit sucks out there." Bren took another drink, letting the alcohol dull his memory.

"You're not in therapy?"

"What the fuck is therapy going to do for me? I know why I can't leave the house. I'm safe here, and the world isn't safe out there. It's not rocket science."

They sat in silence for several minutes, contemplating, drinking, and contemplating about drinking more. Anthony sneezed, a byproduct of sitting in the chairs no one had been anywhere near in years. The cushions had that musty smell of age, and their pattern, once blue checkerboard, had faded to almost nothingness.

Bren's leg started to bounce. He hated awkward stillness. No one except Patrick ever came over to the house. He didn't have to entertain and no longer had the skills anyway. God, he'd been alone for so fucking long.

Anthony looked anywhere but at him, taking in the dusty, generic artwork on the wall and the dingy knickknack things in the shelves next to the table. Once, this had been one of the centerpieces of their house. They'd sit down at the table with their parents and talk about how things went at school. Then, cancer took their mother, a bullet took their father, and indifference took his brother. Now all he had left was the fucking dust.

"I'm done with this awkward shit," Bren said, finishing off his first beer. He stood and walked over to the fridge for another. When he came back, he met Anthony's eyes.

"And?"

"Christ, I don't know. I haven't seen another flesh-and-blood person in so long, I don't know what to do with one. I got cards somewhere, or we could watch mindless afternoon talk shows. Hell, we can fuck. I'm just done sitting here watching the goddamned paint peel."

Anthony stared at him, wide-eyed and shocked.

"What?"

"You want to fuck?"

"Who doesn't? I can get groceries delivered. I can get beer delivered. I can stream porn. Not too many 'hot guy' delivery services in the greater Ferndale area."

Bren didn't bother sitting down at the table with his beer. He turned on his bare heel and began shuffling toward the living room. The bullet hadn't left him with a limp, but his leg twinged enough sometimes that he compensated on his left side.

"Wait," Anthony said before he'd gotten through the kitchen doorway. Bren turned around, and while the kid looked hesitant, there was also a look there he'd seen before. Want. Well, goddamn, someone wanted him. Praise Jesus and hallelujah.

"You want something?"

Anthony's eyes turned dark for a moment, a memory that seemed to cloud his face. Before Bren could ask about it, the kid shoved past him into the living room and waited near the couch. He took off his thin T-shirt, and it seemed to Bren that he wanted to strip quickly before he lost his nerve.

Bren had no issues with that. He watched as the shirt fell to the floor in a heap next to a pile of clothes. Bren had no idea if they were clean or dirty. Anthony's wiry frame made him seem more boyish without the shirt, but the shy way he looked at Bren from under those long bangs made Bren's cock hard.

"Stop," Bren said as Anthony started to unbutton his jeans. Anthony's hands froze on the little piece of metal, and he didn't bother looking up to meet Bren's gaze.

"Yeah, I figured you wouldn't want me, either."

"What the hell are you talking about? I just wanted to do it myself."

Anthony lifted his head at that. "What?"

"Come here so I can take your pants off. I wanna see your dick."

"Oh." Anthony took a step closer so they were almost touching. He fingered the sleeve of Bren's T-shirt, all bravado lost in the stalled momentum of his striptease.

ANTHONY

It took Bren less than three seconds to decide to wrap his hand around the back of Anthony's neck and pull him into a hard, hot kiss. His thoughts spiraled when the blood left his brain and rushed to his cock. The way Anthony kissed and touched him seemed more like a dream than reality. The room around him, the hands on his body, the mouth across his, they felt surreal.

Years of space lay between Anthony and Bren's last fuck buddy.

Anthony shied away for a moment but then seemed to find himself and grabbed the hem of Bren's T-shirt, pulling it up. Anthony smelled like sweat and guy—raw and pure. His body was filled out nicely, even if he was almost too thin.

Bren pulled them down onto the couch, and Anthony landed hard, but the couch cushioned him as Bren came down right on top of him. It took a little maneuvering, but Anthony got Bren's sweats down over his ass, and his hard cock slid into Anthony's hand. Bren whimpered, a needy sound against Anthony's throat, the vibrations tingling them both. Anthony ground his hips against Bren's leg, and his quiet little sounds made Bren ache. He'd never had anyone want him like that. Ever.

"Are you sure you're real?" Bren whispered as he moved his hips, thrusting into Anthony's hand. "It feels so fucking good." He jerked the front of Anthony's briefs down and fisted his cock, not matching the rhythm of his hips. They jerked each other in a chaotic mess of movement.

"You feel good too," Anthony admitted, and their mouths crashed together again, swallowing sounds of aching need.

"Top or bott—?" Bren started to ask, only to be interrupted by the doorbell. Anthony tried to pull him back down on top of him, but Bren gave him one last kiss and climbed off the couch. He hiked up his sweats on the way to the door. Over his shoulder, he saw Anthony grab the hem of his briefs. Then he opened the door. The room filled with a long silence as he took in the pair of women in long dresses and pious smiles standing on his porch.

He did the only thing he could.

He snorted.

"You're kidding, right? Okay, well, I'm fucking this guy on the couch right now. Want to try back in, say... half an hour?" Bren looked over at Anthony, giving his still-nearly-naked body a long appraisal. "No, better make it at least ninety minutes. This kid is hot. Then you can come back and tell me all about how my soul needs to be saved."

He closed the door and could only imagine the shell-shocked faces of the innocent church-going visitors outside. He snickered and pulled his sweats down as he came back to the couch, and to Anthony.

"They're gone, but a guy pulled up out front. He's taking equipment out of the truck. We don't have a lot of time." Without another word, Bren dropped to his knees in front of the couch and pulled Anthony's dick into his mouth. A desperate sound escaped Anthony, and a rush of heat and lust swirled across Bren with the force of a category five hurricane. He wondered for just a second if the people outside had heard. Then he decided he didn't care because his brain had shut down in the very best way possible.

Bren's moan reverberated through the room, and he knew it wouldn't take much to get Anthony to come, not with the way they'd been grinding on each other when the savior sisters knocked on the door. To distract himself from the overwhelming need to explode in his own hand, Bren closed his eyes and tightened his lips.

He rubbed the inside of Anthony's thigh with the hand not jerking his cock and then traced over his balls. After a moment, Bren wrapped his free hand around Anthony's dick and stroked, kissing his own hand as Anthony's cock slid in and out of his mouth.

Anthony tried to pull out when he came, but Bren didn't relent. Each spurt into his mouth made him jerk his own cock faster to catch up, to hit the finish line right behind Anthony. Bren released Anthony and pressed his forehead against the smooth, tender skin of Anthony's stomach, turning his face into the warmth as he moaned. Something welled inside Bren as Anthony ran his fingers over his raggedly chopped hair. He thought maybe that touch, even more than the fist around his dick, made him come into his hand.

Bren had just huffed a sigh when the doorbell rang.

"Fuck."

They both got up this time, throwing on the clothes that had been scattered around them in the chaos of their afternoon play. Bren reached the door first, turning quietly to make sure Anthony's clothes were in place before he opened it. A middle-aged bear of a man stood on the porch with a toolbox in hand.

"I'm here to fix the air-conditioning," he said, as though there'd be a rush of workmen in coveralls with their names sewn into the chest coming to his door.

"What do you need?" Bren asked "Billy," according to the name stenciled in clear black letters on his uniform.

"Nothing, really. Just show me where the furnace and AC are. I'll let you know when I have something." The guy looked at Anthony around his shoulder, and Bren put himself between them. He didn't like the predatory gleam in the man's beady little eyes.

"The furnace is in the basement, so I'll take you down. The AC is in the backyard," he groused, and Anthony got out of the way while Bren showed the man downstairs.

It didn't take long for him to point out what the guy needed, something even the broken brother could do. When he came upstairs, he noticed Anthony looking over his movie collection. He'd collected a host of sci-fi and action movies, from *Terminator* to *Alien*.

"One of the things I miss most about Before." Bren's voice startled Anthony, and he looked up to see Bren nodding toward the movies. "Now, I can't stand the violence."

Anthony nodded and then continued looking at the movies, not meeting Bren's gaze as he spoke.

"Thank you for... uhm... before. I'd never—" Red suffused the back of his neck, cutting off his admission, and he went back to studying the movies.

"You'd never had a blowjob before?" Bren asked gently.

"No. I'd given one, but never gotten."

"You must have had shitty boyfriends."

"I've never had a boyfriend."

Bren watched him for a long moment. Then he walked into the kitchen, leaving Anthony alone in the living room for a moment. He returned with two beers and handed one to Anthony.

"To afternoon blowjobs, hopefully the first of many."

Anthony laughed, and Bren decided he really liked that sound. "Cheers."

Chapter Eight

After an enormous effort of will, Anthony figured out he could get from the liquor store to Bren's house with a combination of the bus and good old-fashioned walking. He probably should have called first, but he didn't have a phone and wasn't sure Bren would want the company. Though he couldn't exactly say why, since all they'd done the day before was bicker and get off, Anthony wanted to see Bren.

The last half block seemed too short to Anthony, and before he could prepare himself for what Bren might say, he knocked on the door. It took a long time for Bren to answer, and Anthony nearly turned around and got back on the bus. After five minutes or so, he knocked again. It wasn't as though Bren would be out. He could have been asleep. If that were the case, unless he snoozed on the couch, the knock wouldn't wake him.

Thirty seconds later, the door flew open, and Bren's red-rimmed eyes focused on him. The stare nearly pushed him back down the stairs, but he tightened his hand on the railing.

"What are you doing here? My brother send you for more babysitting?" Bren growled out the questions, anger spilling through each word.

"No, you said you liked movies. So I brought one without guns. I thought maybe we could grab a pizza and watch it." Anthony didn't back down from Bren's glare but waited for him to weigh the pros and cons of pizza and a movie against more booze.

"What movie?"

"*Harry Potter.*"

"Which one?"

"All of them." Anthony held up the backpack he'd been carrying. He'd brought precious few things with him when he left his parents' house. Every possession he owned vied for space in his car, from books to movies to video games. In the end, he decided he couldn't live without his Harry Potter books and movies. They gave him solace in the darkness when nothing else did.

"I suppose you're going to tell me you have a fucking pizza in that backpack too?" Bren asked but stepped back and let Anthony come into the living room.

"No. I thought about picking it up first, but that's a long fucking walk from the bus stop."

"You took the bus? Are you out of your fucking mind?" Bren took a step closer to him, but Anthony stood his ground.

"I have no car. I wasn't about to ask Patrick to bring me over here because then he'd ask why. The bus was my only option."

"Okay, so since my brother won't be asking, I will. Why?"

"I don't know, to be honest. You're angry and kind of a dick, but sometimes you're funny and you give good head."

"Good enough. What do you want on your pizza?"

And just like that, Anthony stepped into Bren's life.

He dropped the backpack on one of the chairs, and Bren came back from the kitchen with the cordless phone.

"I like any kind of meat," Anthony commented over his shoulder as he dug the movies out of his bag.

"I bet you do."

"Whore. You know what I mean."

"Sausage okay for you? A big one?"

"You're making me regret hiking my way over here."

"Fine, sausage and pepperoni? You want anything else? Wings or something?" Anthony noticed Bren's tone had lost its sharpness.

"I'd love a Pepsi or Coke or whatever."

"I don't have either of those, so I'll order it with the pizza."

"Let me know how much it is. I have cash." Anthony started to pull his wallet out of his back pocket.

"Nah, you brought the movies. This one's on me."

Anthony smiled into his shirt as he went back to dragging the DVDs out of his bag. He flipped through for the first and second movies, unsure how long Bren would be hospitable, and zipped the rest away. He had the DVD menu screen up when Bren came back into the room.

"Should be about forty-five minutes. They have pretty good pizza. I hope it's up to your Chicago standards."

"I didn't live *in* Chicago," Anthony admitted. "I lived in a suburb about an hour or so outside the city. I've never even been to Chicago. I just drove past it on my way here."

"All those years outside the city and you never went into it?"

"After my brother got hurt, we never did anything. We definitely never went downtown to museums or the zoo or whatever. Most of the time, I just stayed in the basement unless Allen and I were playing video games."

"That's a hard way to grow up."

"I didn't have any other options."

"Who's Allen?" Bren asked, settling in to his place on the couch.

"My other brother."

"So what made you pick Detroit? You said you had a friend here, right? Why aren't you with him?"

"I don't know. He hasn't answered any of my messages." Anthony shrugged.

"That's fucked up. You came all the way out here to see him, and he just disappeared?"

"That's what it looks like."

They were quiet for several minutes, and Anthony could hear the clock on the bookshelf ticking away the minutes of awkwardness between them. Finally, Bren tossed a remote at him.

"Come on, boy, you promised me a movie. Are we going to do this or what?"

Anthony laughed and started the DVD. Through a lot of the scenes, Bren asked questions and Anthony explained the things that weren't in the movie. He explained about different relationships and how the magic didn't quite work the same as it did in the book. They'd just started to get into the moving staircases when the doorbell rang and Bren got up to grab the pizza.

They ate off paper towels. Bren had a beer while Anthony stuck with the Pepsi. A quiet sort of calm rested over the room. Just two guys hanging out. It wasn't like their lives were so fucked up they couldn't stand it, right?

"Can I ask you something?" Anthony asked as he wiped hot cheese and sauce from the corner of his mouth with a finger. Bren watched the finger as Anthony popped it into his mouth, and the temperature in the room jumped ten degrees.

"Sure. Not sure if I'll answer, but you can ask whatever." Bren grabbed another slice from the cardboard box and shoved the end into his mouth.

"How did you figure out you couldn't go outside?"

"I don't know, to be honest. When I open the door, I get a fuzzy feeling of anxiety. If I try to step onto the porch, I can't breathe. It's like a panic attack, only I don't know what I'm fucking scared of. When I come back in the house, I'm covered in a cold sweat, but I can take a full breath. Why do you keep fucking asking?"

"My brother had problems like that for a while. Then he found a therapist he liked and slowly he was able to start to control what set him off. Have you ever thought about seeing someone?"

"And how exactly do I go to the shrink's office, pray tell?" Bren asked, and the anger swelled in his voice like a tide. Anthony let it wash over him and continued.

"If you called someone, maybe they could stop by or do something over Skype. You can't be the only person on earth who has an issue leaving their house."

"I don't want to talk to someone. I don't want to relive the shit in my head over and over. I don't want to see it when it's fucking there."

"I was just trying to—"

"Can you just start the fucking movie again?"

Anthony hit the Play button and Hogwarts came back on the screen in all its magical wonder. They sat side by side, finishing their pizza, drinking, and being resolutely quiet. Anthony didn't know how to bridge the gap that seemed to grow on the couch between them. He switched to beer before the brave little wizards dropped through the trap door.

Halfway through his fifth beer of the day, Bren slipped sideways on the couch and put his head on Anthony's shoulder. The warmth of Bren's breath against Anthony's skin gave him goose bumps, but he didn't shiver. He didn't want to do anything to make Bren move. That one gesture summed up everything Anthony wanted from another guy—companionship, affection, and closeness.

"I wish I could go outside. I miss the sun," Bren whispered as the final theme came on and the credits started to roll. The words hit Anthony's gut with real pain because he had no idea how to help.

"I wish you could too," Anthony whispered back.

"I hate being here alone all the time." Bren sat up just enough to capture his lips in a beer-laden, pizza-infused kiss.

"You're not alone." Anthony stroked his cheek once with shaking fingers.

"Jesus, you're beautiful."

"Guys aren't beautiful, are they? That's a chick thing."

"You are."

Anthony cleared his throat. No one had ever called him beautiful before. He couldn't even remember his mother calling him that when he was little. It kindled a warm spot in him.

"You want to watch the next movie?"

"Yeah. I'm mellow and the shit in my head is quiet for the moment. I don't know if it's the beer or if it's you. Usually it never goes away. I'll take it, though." Bren pulled himself up and then nestled in the corner of the couch, bringing Anthony back against his chest. He didn't wrap his arms around Anthony's waist, but just the feeling of Bren's chest against his back gave Anthony a sense of being protected and cared for in a way he'd never felt before.

Even when the movie started and Hedwig came on the screen in her tiny little cage, Anthony felt free for the first time in years.

Chapter Nine

Patrick stood inside his walk-in closet trying to decide which of his pitiful shirts to wear out to dinner with Danielle. The clientele at the liquor store required nothing more than a T-shirt and jeans each day. Sometimes he wore a polo shirt, but he didn't think he even owned a button-down that fit anymore. Over the last two years, he'd shrunk out of everything but the Walmart jeans he'd bought when his designer jeans would no longer stay around his waist. It wasn't that he couldn't afford nice ones. He just didn't care.

He hadn't been social in so long, he'd forgotten how. Danielle's entire job description revolved around being social. Why his flight attendant, sort-of-girlfriend put up with a hermit sort-of-boyfriend, Patrick would never know. Patrick finally just grabbed his nicest polo shirt. It would swallow him, but if he left it untucked, it wouldn't bunch and might look okay enough for their Saturday night dinner in a chain restaurant.

He'd just finished putting a little product in his overgrown hair when a knock on the front door interrupted him. It would have to be good enough. They'd have dinner, maybe see a movie, and end up back in his bed fucking anyway.

Patrick padded out into the living room in his socks. After checking the peephole and seeing Danielle's pretty face, he opened the door and stood to the side. First, Patrick noticed the grim expression, and then he noticed that Danielle had on sweats and a tank top, hardly dinner attire.

"Did I have the night wrong?" Patrick asked as he closed the door behind her.

"No, but we need to talk."

"Nothing good ever follows that statement." Patrick led the way over to the couch and sat down. He was comforted when Danielle sat in the seat next to him rather than on the chair across the room. She didn't look upset, but more resigned. This conversation would not end well.

"There's no easy way to tell you this, so I'm just going to say it. My hub is changing. I've been promoted to international flights. As soon as I can find a sublet, I'm moving to New York. I'll be flying out of JFK." Danielle took his hand. "I'm sorry. I didn't have any warning. We knew it could happen, and I'd ask you to come with me, but...."

"But I can't leave the store, or my brother," Patrick said, chilled by the flat, cold tone of his own voice. The store tethered every part of his life. It felt like an anchor in a churning sea that buffeted him around like a toy boat on Lake Michigan. He and Danielle had been dating only about a year. He shouldn't be this upset.

"I understand. I really do. We knew it might not go the distance." Patrick took a deep breath and blew it out slowly. He'd practiced that same exercise with Bren so many times. Now he could see what Bren meant when he said it was a useless fucking gesture. "You're going to be so amazing. The world won't know what hit it."

Danielle wrapped her arms tightly around Patrick, lips pressed against his throat. He could smell the subtle perfume she wore as her hair tickled his face

"Sell the store," she whispered. "You need to get out of there before it kills you."

"I can't," Patrick whispered back. It was easier when he couldn't see the disappointment and pity in Danielle's face. "I'm trapped here, but I'm glad you're getting out."

She sighed, and for a moment, something crossed her face, but then it was gone.

"I should go." Danielle sat up. "I don't want to make this harder than it is."

And that was it. In the span of less than two minutes, his life had changed yet again. Five minutes ago, he'd had a girlfriend. He'd had dinner plans. He'd had a shelter from the storm of his life. He'd planned to get laid.

Now he was naked in the dark.

"Yeah." He couldn't think of anything to say that didn't involve begging Danielle to stay and be his real girlfriend or promises to sell the store and go. He couldn't leave Bren, and Bren couldn't leave their parents' house. His precarious psychological stability was wrapped tightly around Patrick and around the store. If Patrick walked away, it would break his brother.

The click of virtual shackles rang louder than the pounding in his ears.

Patrick walked Danielle to the door and received one final peck on the cheek. Then he watched her walk down the stairs and out of his life. They wouldn't keep in touch. Most exes never did. He wouldn't laugh at Danielle's corny puns or share a quick fuck with her ever again.

Patrick shook his head to clear the ringing in his ears, but it persisted. The hollow, trapped, panicky feeling in his chest did too. His palms sweated when he grabbed the keys to the RAV4 off the small table next to the door. The pressure on his chest didn't let up as he pulled the driver's-side door closed beside him.

He was sick of the expectations, the pain driving a knife into his soul. Only one thing would help him not to think, not to feel. His brother spent half his life drunk because Bren didn't have responsibilities or a noose around his neck. Fuck that.

Patrick turned the keys in the ignition and turned the truck toward the liquor store.

Chapter Ten

Since the liquor store closed early on Sundays, Anthony decided to pick up dinner before close, grab a book, and read. He'd continue with the last *Harry Potter* because it reminded him of his afternoon with Bren. As much as people liked Harry, Anthony identified more with Neville, who started out invisible and ended up instrumental in Voldemort's destruction. Anthony didn't need to save the world, but he'd love to learn how to take off that invisibility cloak.

Then he thought about the one person who didn't see him as invisible and picked up his laptop. God, he loved the memory of lying back against Bren's chest. He'd never had that before. Of course, he couldn't make a big deal out of it. Guys didn't do that, right?

You look cute when you're sleeping.

Yeah, that would do it—casual, but enough to let Bren know he was thinking about their time together. He didn't even know what was going on with them, but this shit was exhausting.

The last slice of pizza sat like a challenge on the cardboard circle at the end of his make-shift bed. He reached for it, and a pain in his stomach stopped him short. Tomorrow, when Patrick got in to the store, he'd ask if he could put a couple of things in the cooler downstairs since he didn't have a refrigerator up there. That way he could save the other half of a pizza, a little money, and his skinny jeans.

His computer dinged with a new message from Bren.

Come over later and you can sleep with me.

A smile spread slowly across his lips and Anthony clicked the reply button. Before he could type the first word, he heard the sound of shattering glass from the store below. Anthony waited a heartbeat, listening hard. Maybe he'd imagined it. He set the book on the sleeping bag and held his breath. Then he heard it again. The bed shifted, and he was on his feet reaching for his shoes when he remembered what Patrick had said about confronting intruders downstairs. Anthony had promised he would stay upstairs and call the police, but if Patrick was down there with his girlfriend again, he didn't want to get anyone in trouble. If he called the police, they might ask things about him. At seventeen, they wouldn't give him much choice about calling his parents. He'd only been in Detroit for a couple weeks, but he felt comfortable.

Another crash, closer to the stairs, and Anthony picked up the portable phone he'd promised to keep with him. It took just a minute to throw on his shoes, and he opened the door to the apartment with silent fingers. The stairs didn't creak as Anthony made his way down them, but he feared someone might hear him breathing, harsh and heavy. It sounded so loud in his ears. If he had to keep creeping down these fucking stairs, he'd have a heart attack.

His feet whispered against the linoleum when he reached the bottom. He looked around the small space, lit only by what came from the overstock room across the short hallway. The miniature bottles of scotch, rum, and gin lined up like little solders on the shelves all around him. He wished for a wand so he could summon them into a tiny liquid army. Anthony nearly screamed when a bottle whizzed past the entrance to the room and exploded against the opposite wall.

"I hate this fucking place," a hoarse voice cried, so full of pain that it made Anthony ache. He straightened and walked out of the room as his fear dissipated. He recognized the voice, and the pain. Patrick stood in the middle of the sales floor, hefting a fifth of Absolut from the display next him. His aim went wild and the bottle crashed against the front of the cooler. Anthony couldn't believe the glass door didn't crack.

He navigated the war zone of glass fragments, puddles of alcohol, and a Kahlúa display lying on its side across the aisle. Coffee grounds and mud-colored mess splattered the surrounding stock.

"Patrick." He tried to make his voice soft so he didn't startle his boss, but it didn't work. Another vodka bottle crashed to the floor as Patrick spun, overbalanced, and toppled to the floor, the knees of his jeans missing the shattered glass by inches. He squinted up and it took a long moment for recognition.

"Hey, kid, what are you doing down here?" With the slur, Anthony had a hard time understanding him.

"Keeping you from destroying stuff. What are you doing?"

Patrick's face darkened, and he glared around at the bottles and cans as if they'd offended him. He tried to stand but stumbled and landed with his back against the base of the counter.

"I hate this place."

"I got that. You were yelling it," Anthony reminded him.

"I was?"

"Yes, when you sent a bottle screaming past my head and it exploded against the wall."

Patrick's expression changed in an instant from anger to horror. He grabbed Anthony's arm and started checking him for injuries.

"Are you okay?"

"Yeah, I'm fine. You were saying, about hating this place," Anthony prompted and knelt so they were at eye level. Patrick's eyes cleared a little and he took a breath.

Patrick slumped back. "I had a life in Ohio. I went to college, had a great job, and a great little place. Don't get me wrong, I loved my dad and brother, but for the first time since Mom died, I'd found some place I belonged. You know?"

Anthony nodded, and Patrick kept talking, his words clearer with focus.

"Bren was going to take care of the store. Dad had someone to pass it down to. Everyone was happy." Patrick's eyes took on a faraway look, and Anthony's stomach clenched. His heart skipped in that way it did before anyone said anything about what really happened to Aaron. He didn't want to hear, but couldn't turn away.

"What happened?" he whispered.

"Fourth of July weekend two years ago, a guy came in with a gun. He robbed the place. My dad and brother were working. I watched the surveillance tapes. They both had their hands up and they weren't anywhere near the guy. It wasn't like they were trying to stop him, but he... he shot them both." Patrick grabbed a half-empty bottle of Jack from the floor and took a swig from it, then he indicated a place on the floor in the middle of the open sales area.

"They went down right there. My dad bled out, and my brother had to watch it happen. It took about fifteen minutes for another customer to come in and call the police, but by then, my dad was already dead."

Anthony put a hand on Patrick's shoulder.

"That's a horrible thing to live with." He didn't say how sorry he was because he fucking hated when people told him that about Aaron. They didn't understand sorry. Anthony, he understood sorry.

"I came home and my brother was a fucking mess. He's still a fucking mess. But they had me and Kevin come in here, step over the blood, and tell them if anything was missing. Tell them how much the guy took from the cash register. Who fucking cares?"

Anthony didn't say anything. He agreed. The amount of money the guy took wouldn't make up for what Patrick's family had suffered.

"I wanted to sell it, but Bren... I needed to give him time to adjust, to see if he'd be up to taking it back. That was two years ago. Two years and nothing has changed. I'm going to be tied to this place for the rest of my fucking life. Bren can't come here, but he also can't let it go. This place meant everything to my dad, especially after Mom died." Patrick's voice was ragged; a hard edge of pain sharpened his words.

"How did your mother die?"

"Cancer."

"My grandma died of cancer a couple years ago. It's not pretty."

"Nope," Patrick said, popping the *p*.

Silence stretched between them for a long time, during which Anthony looked up and down the aisles, assessing the damage. Aside from the display on its side, mostly it appeared Patrick had just been chucking bottles around.

"Why did you run away, Anthony? I mean, I know about your brother, but why leave?"

Patrick's voice was so soft, it barely registered in Anthony's range of hearing, but once he did, he couldn't unhear it. Patrick had told him his damage, so it was Anthony's turn to step up to the plate. He stood and wandered down the big wine aisle to grab a broom and dustpan from hangers on the wall of the overstock room. When he returned less than sixty seconds later, Patrick had slouched even more down the counter. If he could have found something to rest his head on, Anthony figured Patrick would have already have passed out. Not many guys would still be conscious after half a bottle of Jack.

Anthony began sweeping up the coffee grounds and shards of glass from the display. "When I was a kid, about ten, I think I'd just started fifth grade, that's when Aaron was attacked. He was sixteen and probably the coolest person I knew then. Well, except for Allen, our middle brother. He was fourteen then." It helped not to look at Patrick as the words spewed from him like sewer filth. "Aaron was kidnapped. My mom never really explained anything to me, but over the years I picked up bits and pieces. He'd been tortured and raped."

"Anthony—" Patrick started, but Anthony cut him off. If he didn't get it out now, while Patrick's defenses were down and he was only half listening, Anthony would never be able to tell the whole story.

"I remember he was like a completely different person when he came home. In the span of a few weeks, we went from a happy family to not a family at all. Aaron used to wake up screaming all the time and it scared me, so my parents moved Allen and me into rooms in the basement so we couldn't hear Aaron. But we couldn't hear anything else, either. I was just a kid and scared all the time down there, of the dark, of mice, of a fucking monster in my closet. Because by then, I knew there were monsters. One of them had hurt Aaron." He kicked an empty beer case toward the back wall. "Anyway, I hated it. My life was so fucked up. School was a nightmare, and my parents were so focused on Aaron, they didn't have time for me. Then when I was fourteen, Allen went off to college and I was all alone down there. Earlier this year, Aaron moved out too. He found someone to love. He and Spencer are good for each other, I guess."

"Your brother is gay?"

"Yeah. I am too." Anthony looked for any kind of disgust or hatred in Patrick's face, but found nothing but compassion. It was nothing like coming out to Chase. He finally let out the breath he'd been holding on to with everything he had. Patrick must have known about Bren too.

"Okay, so why did you leave?"

"For months before graduation, my parents kept telling me that I had to go to college, but high school was so awful, I didn't want to. They said even Aaron went to college. Perfect fucking Aaron."

"I still don't see—"

"The night before I left, I went to a party with some people from school and Chase. He was my best friend. And it was... It...." The tears finally fell, and Anthony wiped them away with an angry swipe of his t-shirt.

"Come here," Patrick whispered. Anthony propped the broom against the shelves and took a few steps toward Patrick, who grabbed Anthony's hand and pulled him down onto the floor next to him. Startled, Anthony tried to struggle, but Patrick just put an arm around him in kind of a half-straight guy hug. God, it was amazing. So fucking amazing. He took advantage of Patrick's blood alcohol level and rested his head on the man's broad shoulder.

"It was so awful. We were in the bedroom and it was great and we were finally together the way I'd always wanted. I... I sucked him off, but then he got really mean."

"Did he hurt you?" Patrick's arm tightened around him, and he felt safe for the first time in nearly a decade.

"Not like that. He called me a fag and then told everyone at the party I'd blown him. When I got home, I was shaking. I got on the Xbox and Jay started talking to me. He invited me to Detroit. That was at like three in the morning. By eleven, I was on the road. I don't even know what happened."

"Do you want to go back? I'm sure your parents would help with the car."

The reluctance in Patrick's voice surprised Anthony, and he shook his head. "No. I've been happier the last two weeks than I have been in a long time. I mean, I have to be really careful with money and make my own way, but it feels like someone took a really heavy chain off my neck." Anthony whispered the words into the darkness, finally able to say it.

"I know how that chain feels."

They sat like that for a bit, just sharing the weight of their lives. Patrick smelled like sweat and booze, but he wasn't alone anymore. Cars passed outside the plate-glass window and Anthony was fine letting the world go by. He was comfortable and happy. Until Patrick started to slide farther down the counter, his head drooping onto Anthony's cheek.

"Okay, you're too big for me to get up the stairs. I'm going to go get the mattress and bring it down here. We can sleep in the stockroom." Anthony stood up, hating the loss of Patrick's warmth.

"No, I should just go home."

"There is no way I'm letting you drive. You drank at least half a fifth of Jack, and you can't even keep your eyes open. And I can't drive you because I don't know where you live. You're in no condition to give directions. Just sit here. If you pass out, don't fall on the floor. I'll be right back."

Patrick made an undecipherable sound that Anthony took for agreement. He pushed Patrick upright once more and sprinted for the stairs. It took a few minutes for him to figure out how to disconnect the pump attached to the inflatable mattress, but eventually he got both mattress and pump downstairs into the back room. He unplugged the small radio sitting on the scotch shelf and shoved the plug for the pump into the socket. The steady hum of the pump drowned out even the compressors in the cooler, but after the amount of liquor Patrick had, he'd probably sleep through an earthquake. Anthony just hoped he hadn't started yet.

ANTHONY

Patrick's eyes drooped and then shot open again as Anthony came back up the aisle.

"Okay, come on, let's get you back on the mattress."

"You don't have to—"

"You've been taking care of me for weeks now. Let me return the favor."

"I... okay." Patrick sank farther, and Anthony bent his knees, locked his arms under Patrick's, and helped lift him off the floor. Their bodies aligned, hips, chests, and legs, and Anthony felt it everywhere. He tried not to think about his straight boss pressed against him, but his seventeen-year-old body had a mind of its own.

"Okay, one step and then... the next... good." Anthony grunted as he ignored the need in his dick; a need that thinking of Bren only made worse. Anthony had stopped by for another movie the Friday before, but they hadn't fucked around again. It made him edgy.

Anthony half carried, half dragged his drunk boss down an aisle not big enough for two grown men. They stumbled near the margarita mix. A bottle crashed to the floor when Patrick grabbed the shelf for support. Anthony had to turn them sideways when he reached the coolers, and Patrick crowded against him. He turned his head away from the stench of Patrick's booze breath, but the friction of their bodies rubbing as he slid them through the doorway more than made up for the smell of Jack Daniels mixed with what smelled like wet dog and maybe even the ass of a dead rhino.

The wind left his lungs when his feet slid on the wet floor and his back slammed against the side of the cooler. Patrick's hard body pressed against him, and it took a second in the dizzying tumble of arms and legs slammed against the wall to notice Patrick's hips moving against him.

They broke apart at the sound of a shrill ring in Patrick's back pocket. Since his hands were already there, Anthony plucked a cell phone from the left side and held it up. Patrick didn't even look at it, he just swiped his finger across the front and screamed into it.

"No, Bren!" He slammed his finger onto every pixel around the smartphone's surface without actually hitting the End button. Anthony pressed it for him and slid the cell phone into his own pocket. It killed him to hear the pain in Patrick's voice, especially directed at Bren. But he could only take care of one of them at a time.

The cell phone provided a perfect distraction, and he hobbled the few remaining steps into the stockroom and lowered Patrick less than gracefully onto the mattress. Kneeling at the bottom of the mattress, he grabbed first one leather dress shoe and then the other and popped them off. He let them fall near a full case of Smirnoff. His breath caught when he saw Patrick reach for his belt.

"You do have something on under your jeans right?"

"Yeah. I think I have an undershirt on too. Does it bother you?"

"No, I guess not, but I have to sleep there too, so don't get naked. You *are* my boss."

Patrick succeeded in unbuckling his belt and opening the front of his jeans but lost the battle trying to get them down. Anthony pulled on his arm and got him to sit up in an awkward position perched on the side of the inflated bed. The shirt came off easily enough when Patrick decided to lift his arms over his head. He complained about the room spinning after the shirt lay on the floor. Anthony grabbed the waistband of Patrick's jeans and told him to lift up, which he managed.

Anthony pulled off his own shoes and jeans, leaving the T-shirt to cover at least part of his underwear. He went around to the other side of the mattress but came back when he noticed Patrick still sitting up on the side.

"Come on, lie down so we can get some sleep," Anthony whispered, though there was no one anywhere in the store to hear him. He pushed back on the man's shoulder, and he fell backward, lengthwise across the bed.

"Well, that didn't work as well as I'd hoped," he grumbled. "Come on, man, help me out. Turn toward the pillows." He grabbed Patrick's shoulders and manhandled him onto one of the bare pillows. Then Anthony lifted Patrick's feet from the floor in his twisted position.

He didn't want to think about the stuff collecting on the bottom of his socks as he moved over to the other side of the mattress and climbed on carefully. If he simply dropped onto it, the force would shoot Patrick out into the floor. As funny as that would have been, he didn't want to haul the man back into bed again. Anthony jerked the covers up over them and snuggled down. The temperature downstairs certainly registered far lower than upstairs.

"You still awake?" Anthony murmured to the darkness.

"Almost," Patrick responded.

"What happened tonight that upset you so badly?" He reached over and touched Patrick's arm, squeaking when the arm closed in over him.

"Danielle dumped me."

"Your girlfriend?"

"Yeah."

"I'm sorry."

He felt Patrick shrug, but the arm stayed around him. Anthony decided it could stay there. Patrick wouldn't remember anyway.

"Nor your fault. She got transferred to New York and I couldn't go with her. We hadn't been together a year. It's not like we were going to get married or anything."

"I would guess that it still hurts."

"You ever had a boyfriend?"

"No. No one ever wanted me."

Patrick shifted and finally let go of Anthony, settling into the bed and closing his eyes.

"Well, I'm glad you're here."

Chapter Eleven

The shrill ring of his cell phone crashed against Patrick's temples with the force of a sledgehammer. He tried to roll over but couldn't get any leverage with the body half on his. Patrick's dick tried to show some enthusiasm at Danielle's proximity, but the inside of his mouth tasted like a rabid hamster's cage. No morning fuck for them.

As the shroud of unconsciousness rolled away, his stomach recoiled. He took several long, deep breaths to try to stop the onslaught of his stomach contents from spewing over the bed. When he cracked one eye open, the cooler in front of his face confused him. Nothing made sense. He had no memory of the night before and was almost afraid to turn his head and see who lay in the bed beside him.

Like bad cable reception, pictures started to form in his head: getting dressed for his date, Danielle sitting on the couch, and then the drive to the store. They were broken and warped leading into the eye of the storm: smashing bottles, screaming, Anthony.

Anthony.

The mattress beneath him felt like the inflatable kind, like the one from upstairs, the one Anthony slept on. He couldn't think about it anymore. Patrick didn't go to bed with a seventeen-year-old. He certainly didn't go to bed with a seventeen-year-old *boy*. Even drunk, he couldn't have strayed that far into insanity.

"Are you awake?" a timid voice whispered in the darkness.

Oh fuck.

That's exactly what I did.

"Yeah," he managed, a wall of regret and pain stacking brick by brick in his chest. Patrick cracked an eye open. A mass of soft, shaggy brown hair filled his vision, and he took another long breath.

"How are you feeling?"

"I don't know yet," he said honestly. "I think that depends on if either of us are naked."

"Neither of us are naked."

"Thank fuck for that."

A long pause stretched the air between them. Patrick felt the tenuous mattress shift violently, and the warm weight across his chest and arm disappeared.

"Well, thanks for that ego boost," Anthony said.

Patrick's eyes were open just far enough to see Anthony grab a discarded pair of jeans off a nearby case of... something, he couldn't tell what. Then he threw on a pair of shoes without bothering to tie them and stalked toward the pint room and the stairs beyond. Patrick tried to sit up, to follow, but his hangover slammed him back down onto the mattress with the force of a giant, invisible anvil.

He closed his eyes and took stock, tried to formulate a plan, but his brain battered the inside of his skull. Everything seemed so far away: the john, the bottles of water in the cooler, and especially the container of aspirin in his desk drawer. He'd have to crawl across the Sahara to reach any of it. Somewhere above his head, he heard the cooler door open and close, but he couldn't make sense out of it. Then he heard it again. Before Patrick could turn his head to look, a bottle of water appeared from thin air, dangling in front of his face like a mirage.

"Here. I brought you some Tylenol too," Anthony said. "I've had my share of hangovers and they suck."

"You're seventeen, how could you have had your share of hangovers?"

Anthony snorted and pushed the bottle closer to Patrick's face.

"I've known my way around a bottle since I was about twelve."

ANTHONY

Patrick didn't say anything to that. Nothing filtering into his head at that moment made any sense, so he decided to deal with it when his brain stopped trying to claw its way out of his ear. When he took the open bottle of water, Anthony dropped three pills into his other palm. He didn't question; he just swallowed them.

Time didn't have the same meaning in his head as it did on the clock. When he checked the round monstrosity on the wall, ten a.m. seemed so fucking early. He could have just lain down in the last fifteen minutes or so. Instead, it would be time to open the store soon for Kevin because the pop-up reminder on his phone indicated he and Danielle were supposed to be at Sandy's for a backyard barbecue today. If he called and cancelled, especially after waking Sandy up last week to help the kid, she'd murder him.

"Anthony?" he mumbled, trying not to let the sound rattle around too much in his head.

"Yeah?"

Patrick took a chance and lifted his head. The ache sent him crashing back down onto the makeshift bed. Instead, he lifted an arm. Yes, that worked a little better. He waved Anthony over and took his other hand off his eyes. The room came into focus again, still dark, *Thank you God.* The bed dipped next to him.

"I'm going to Sandy's for a cookout today. Would you like to come with me?"

Silence stretched between them as Anthony considered his answer. Patrick turned his head to the side, trying not to vomit all over the only bed Anthony had. He took a slow, deep breath in through his nose and blew it out through his mouth.

"They won't want me there." Anthony's whisper barely registered over the roar of the cooler mechanics.

Patrick forced himself into a sitting position with his legs stretched out in front of him on the inflated surface. Turning his body to face Anthony took too much effort, so he merely shifted so he could see the boy wrapped around himself as he huddled at the top of the bed, his back resting against the shelves of booze and his knees pressed to his thin chest. Overgrown hair hung in his eyes.

"Of course they do. So do I."

"Why?"

"I want you to come with me. You can't spend all your time cooped up in this store." Patrick rested a hand on Anthony's arm.

"People never seem to like me very much."

"I like you. Come on, I need to call my brother and then stop by my place and shower. You wanna run upstairs and get ready while I do that?"

"I don't have anything nice—"

"Shorts and a T-shirt will work just fine, kid. There's no need to impress." Patrick smiled a watery kind of half grin through the pain radiating through his temples. He wanted to go home and spend the day in bed, but he owed Sandy for coming to look at Anthony's car. Plus, he had to tell Sandy about him and Danielle before she heard it somewhere else, or they'd never find his body.

"I... whatever," Anthony said finally. It took the kid a long time to unlock the arms wrapped around his gangly legs and stand, but eventually, he climbed off the bed. Patrick watched and expected him to head straight upstairs, but instead he leaned over one of the boxes to grab something off the vodka overstock shelf. He held it out wordlessly and Patrick recognized it as his cell phone.

"Do I want to know how you ended up with my cell phone?"

"Your brother called and you yelled at him. I took it to keep you from throwing it against the wall."

"Thank you. I appreciate that."

Damn, now he really had to call Bren.

After a long and expansive sigh that made his head throb, Patrick pressed the speed dial and called his brother. With each ring, his heart grew heavier. He didn't remember Bren calling the night before or what he might have said, but it couldn't have been kind. When the lifeless automated voice told him he'd reached voice mail for the third time, Patrick hung up and tried a different tactic. He switched to text instead.

I know you probably don't want to talk to me right now, but I'm sorry about last night. I promised you I wouldn't turn off the cameras so I'm sure you saw it all. The kid said you called and I yelled at you. I don't remember it, but I'm sure I was an asshole. I'm sorry.

The screen stayed blank for a long time, long enough for Patrick's heart to pound with adrenaline-spiked fear. He didn't want to think about Bren not being able to forgive him, or.... No. No, nothing had happened to Bren. He was fine, just stubborn.

He thanked God when his phone chimed with a text notification from Bren and slid his thumb across the screen to open it.

Smash it all. I don't give a fuck. Asking you to stay and help was asking too much. Sell it and go.

The text hurt like a physical blow, a slap to the face. Bren didn't want him there anymore. It was a blessing and a curse rolled up into one tightly wrapped, fucked-up little package. He could have his life back, but he'd only have it without Bren, his only family. No. No way that would happen.

When he glanced up, Anthony had come downstairs, his lanky body fit into a pair of loose jeans with a T-shirt, looking every bit like the scared, lost boy he was. *The boy who took care of your drunken ass last night, and the boy who slept in your bed.*

"Okay, let's try that again since you didn't hear me the first time." Anthony took a step forward. "Are you okay?" Water glistened in his hair and spotted a few places on his light-colored shirt.

"My brother hates me," Patrick said, looking away from the compassion in Anthony's gaze. He didn't deserve compassion. Bren needed him, and he'd let his brother down. He felt sick.

"My brother hates me too; I know how that feels." Anthony shrugged. "You get used to it and you go on with your life."

Patrick squinted up at Anthony. "Have you ever tried to fix it?"

"I don't want to fix it. The feeling is pretty mutual. But your brother doesn't hate you. He's just pissed off."

Patrick sighed and let his head fall back. He spoke to the ceiling. "Let's go over to Sandy's place. I'll stop by after that and see him, give him some time to cool off."

"You're sure it's okay that I go?"

"I want you to go. Does that help?"

"Yeah," Anthony murmured. Patrick wasn't sure if he was supposed to hear it, but it tugged at something in him.

"Sean should be there, the stocker you took over for. He's Sandy's cousin. That's how he got a job at the store. So you'll have someone your age there."

Patrick realized, too late, that judging from Anthony's glare, he'd said the wrong thing.

"I just meant that maybe you won't feel so out of place with strangers." Patrick rubbed his temples and wished with all his might that the Tylenol would kick in. He couldn't think with his head throbbing in time with the band marching around inside it. "Christ, cut me some slack, my head is going to fall off. I don't need anyone else mad at me right now, though I seem to be doing a spectacular job of pissing people off today."

"Whatever."

"Fabulous. I need to stop by the house first and shower. Are you ready?"

"Yeah."

As Anthony grabbed his shoes from the floor, Patrick wondered if the kid knew another word. "Yeah" seemed to be his default answer. Instead of commenting further, he swiped his thumb across the phone he still held and started a text to Sandy.

Small change of plans. I'm bringing the kid instead of Danielle. I'll explain when I get there.

They were climbing into the RAV4 when he got a response.

I wanted you to bring the kid anyway.

"Sandy said she wanted me to bring you anyway." Patrick held the phone up and waved it at Anthony, not so he could read it, but to illustrate the point. The sunshine that broke through the clouds in Anthony's eyes made him want to kiss Sandy. He didn't get to see Anthony smile often, but it made him happy.

"That was really nice." Anthony pushed his chestnut hair away from his eyes and smiled a shy, secretive smile.

"Sandy is good people, and her husband is a great cook. It's got to be better than the takeout you've been living on for weeks."

"I don't know. That pizza place has pretty good food, and it's cheap. I don't mind so much."

Patrick pulled out of the parking lot and headed toward the townhouse. He'd rented it on a whim when he got back to Detroit, thinking he'd only need it for six months, maybe a year. He'd just signed his third lease last month, so Bren was shit out of luck if he expected Patrick to leave. He'd have to pay two months' rent if he broke the lease.

The silence in the RAV turned painful at the last stoplight, almost as bad as the headache pounding in his temples. "Have you heard from anyone back home?" Patrick asked, grasping at straws for a topic of conversation.

"I haven't checked. I look for emails from Jay, but nothing."

"You said you have two brothers, right?" Patrick asked. Anthony nodded and kept his gaze focused out the passenger window. "Have you heard from the other one?"

"Yeah. He's pissed at me."

"Because you left?"

"Probably. He told me to come down to Indianapolis and stay with him if I didn't want to stay with our parents, but I can't exactly do that. Plus it's his girlfriend's place. Totally awk."

"Yeah, at least here you have the entire apartment to yourself. Even if it's not much of one." Something in his gut told him that wasn't the whole story, but he didn't press. He wanted to help Anthony settle there. Maybe it was just selfish. If he couldn't leave, he wanted someone to stay with him.

"And I don't have to listen to people doing it at all hours... oh wait." Anthony smirked.

"Oh damn, you didn't?"

"Yep. I heard something and thought someone was breaking into the store, so I came downstairs. I grabbed a bottle to defend myself and, well... I'm sure you know what I saw."

"Oh God." Patrick would have put his hands over his face if he weren't driving. "I'm so sorry, Anthony. I shouldn't have put you in that position."

"It wasn't my position that was an issue," Anthony said with a laugh.

"Point taken, but still...."

"Besides, it was hot."

Patrick couldn't have hear that right. "I'm sorry?"

"I've never done that. I've seen some porn, but I've never seen two people having sex right in front of me. It was kinda hot, even if it was a chick." Anthony's fair skin reddened from the top of his T-shirt to his hairline, but he kept up the bravado.

Patrick couldn't go along with it. He couldn't talk to this kid about bending Danielle over some cases of beer and fucking her. Though he'd be lying if he said it didn't turn him on to know Anthony had watched from the shadows. He hated the depravity of it, but apparently, depravity was the new black.

"So, uh, you said you were going to turn eighteen soon, right?"

Anthony laughed at that. He sat with his foot pulled up onto the seat and his thin fingers wrapped around the back of his neck, his black, chipped nails barely visible.

"I'm legal in about ten days."

"It has nothing to do with you being legal. I was just curious."

"Sure."

Patrick peeked over to see a wry grin on Anthony's face and couldn't help the answering expression on his own. They pulled up to the townhouse, and Patrick climbed out and made it halfway up the walk before he realized Anthony wasn't behind him. He turned to see him watching through the windshield, his face a mask of hesitation.

"You can stay there if you want, or you can come in the house." He waited. Either the boy trusted him, or he didn't. It took a long time for him to reach over that four inches and open the door. It took even longer for him to take the same half dozen steps up the drive Patrick had made.

"You could have stayed in the car."

"Yeah, but it smells like cheese."

"Like the good kind of cheese you put on fries with chili?" Patrick asked.

"No, more like the stuff you find behind the couch after a week or two."

"Ew."

"No kidding."

Patrick glanced over his shoulder to make sure Anthony followed him up the trio of stairs to his front door. He unlocked the door and held it open behind him.

"Help yourself to anything in the kitchen. I'm sure you're hungry. I'm going to go upstairs for a quick shower, and then we can take off."

"You're gonna dress after that shower, right?" Anthony asked with a raised eyebrow. Patrick laughed, feeling a little lighter than he had in days.

"Maybe."

"Good enough."

Chapter Twelve

Anthony wandered through the downstairs of Patrick's townhouse. He found a wraparound couch set off by waist-high speakers on either side of the enormous sixty-inch television on the wall. He kept walking, past bookcases lined with movies, and stopped in front of the entertainment center. An Xbox 360 sat in a place of honor in the center, flanked by the cable box and a Blu-ray player. Maybe sometime he should see if Patrick would let him come over and log into the Xbox with his profile. Maybe he could get Jay to talk to him. It wasn't even that he wanted to live with Jay anymore. He liked Patrick. He liked being on his own. He liked working toward something. In his parents' basement, he had everything he could have ever wanted, everything except friends and purpose.

Anthony just wanted to know what the fuck was going on.

The matchbox kitchen didn't really match the rest of the townhouse. It was barely large enough to turn around in. He liked it. The stainless-steel appliances looked good against the backdrop of modern glass-fronted cabinets. Anthony opened the refrigerator to see if Patrick had water and found a couple of six-packs of beer bottles instead. His boss didn't seem to be a stranger to booze, just like Anthony. But as that thought sunk in, another one blazed bright across his mind.

For the first time in his life last night, Anthony had taken care of someone else—not his parents, not Allen, not even Saint Aaron, but him. He liked the strength that filled his bones. Anthony wasn't useless as everyone had supposed. Maybe he really could figure out his life.

"Hey," Patrick said from the doorway with a small smile... and no shirt.

"Hey."

"What was that weird look?" Patrick asked as he pulled a T-shirt over his head. His long, lean ab muscles flexed against the waistband of his jeans.

"I.... Nothing. Did you hear from your brother?"

"No. Not since he told me to fuck off, sell the store, and get out of his life."

"Do you want to stop over there on the way to the cookout?" Anthony asked. He wanted to check on Bren just as much as Patrick did. Something inside of him ached at the thought of Bren in pain.

"No, let's save the unpleasantness for after. Sandy invited him too, but unless we had the cookout in his living room...."

"My brother Aaron was like that for a long time. Living your life around that is exhausting."

"Yeah, it really is."

FIFTEEN MINUTES LATER, they pulled up in front of Sandy's place, and Anthony whistled. There, sitting in the driveway were two vintage cars, the bodywork and paint so perfect they appeared brand new. Sunlight gleamed in all the right places from the early summer day. Anthony didn't know anything about cars, though he tried to keep the Mustang in shape at Allen's insistence. But the ones sitting in the drive, those were worth getting excited over. When he glanced up, Patrick grinned at him.

"Restoring cars is kind of a hobby for Sandy and her husband, Butch."

"Butch? Really?" Anthony snorted and reached for the handle.

"He's got a name, but after all these years, I'm not even sure I ever knew what it was. We always just called him Butch. You'll see. He's like a fucking mountain."

They climbed out of the car. Anthony grabbed the bag of ice he'd insisted Patrick let him buy. He couldn't show up with absolutely nothing. His mother would die. That twinge in his chest slammed into him again at the thought of his mother, but he ignored it. Patrick carried the plates and cups he'd bought, and they headed not to the front door as Anthony expected, but to a side gate.

On the other side of the fence, the world opened up onto a yard full of people in small groups, islands of humanity pocketed around tables and clusters of camp chairs. He saw Sandy right away, carrying a tray toward a house of a man next to the grill. Six and a half feet tall and as wide as Anthony and Patrick put together, that had to be Butch. He grinned at Sandy and exchanged the tray for a kiss. Anthony recognized no one and had turned to stand next to the fence out of the way when a voice stopped him.

"Hey, Patrick!"

A guy not much older than Anthony with a thin face and a friendly expression popped up next to them and smiled at Patrick. His hair, shaved on the sides with longer blond waves on top, fell into his eyes, and he flipped it back.

"Sean, how you doin' kid? This is Anthony, our new stocker."

"Not much of a kid anymore, man," he said with a laugh. "But it looks like you replaced me with one. Is he even old enough to have a job?"

The smile never left Sean's face, but something in Patrick's expression faltered when he looked at Anthony. He had to see the storms brewing inside, the ones Anthony could never hide.

"Anthony's tougher than he looks. He lives on his own and has done a fair job of settling in."

Patrick turned his head toward Sean and whispered something. Anthony caught only the word *alone* spoken in concern. Then he brushed his hand over his stomach the way he always seemed to do when there was something on his mind. Like absent crumbs of thought had landed on his shirt.

"Hey, Anthony." Sean motioned to his friends from the door. "These are my friends Jeff and Chris." Sean grinned. "Man, Boss Man didn't even wait for the body to get cold before he gave my job away. How do you like working for this guy?" He threw a thumb over his shoulder at Patrick, who smiled.

"He hasn't tied me up in the stockroom or anything… yet."

"I thought I was the only one you tied up in the stockroom," Sean said, throwing a wink at Patrick. A blush suffused Patrick's face, and he coughed the embarrassment out of his throat.

"You keep guys tied up in the stockroom? I thought you just slept with them there. But then again, I thought you were straight," Anthony said with wry amusement.

Patrick flushed again, and Anthony laughed while Sean watched them with interest. The way Patrick kept losing eye contact with him told Anthony he'd flustered his boss. After last night, he figured he had some freedom to tease Patrick.

"You slept with a guy in the stockroom?" Sean asked.

Patrick glared at Anthony.

"You're fired," he said.

Anthony's heart caught in his throat, afraid that maybe he'd gone too far. Then he saw the joke dancing in Patrick's eyes.

"No, I'm not."

"No, you're not." Patrick turned back to Sean. "Stop ganging up on me," he warned. "I want him to keep working here for a while since you decided to desert me."

"Aw, don't be like that. If I hadn't had to take that extra night class to graduate, I'd still be working there."

"Sure, sure...."

"Hey, by the way, the scholarship came through, so my bachelor's should be easier than the associate was."

"That's awesome, Sean. I told you that you could do it. So, what are you guys up to?" Patrick brushed the nonexistent whatever off the front of his shirt for the hundredth time this week. Anthony wondered what the hell it was.

"After this, we're gonna pick up some beer and going over to Chris's apartment to play games. Wanna come hang out?" Sean asked. Anthony looked away. Clearly, he wasn't included in the invitation, except maybe as an afterthought because he was standing next to Patrick. Awkwardness crept in, surrounded by the smell of backyard barbecue.

"I'm gonna head over to Bren's after this. He's pissed at me. What about you, Anthony? You could go with them. I'm sure Sean would give you a ride back to the store."

Anthony could hear the disguised plea in his voice. *Please get this kid away from me for a while.* He simply watched them. Sean had invited Anthony for Patrick's sake, not because he'd wanted to. Fuck that. He didn't need a pity friend. Now he understood why Bren didn't want to leave the house, and he wished more than anything he was there watching a movie with him.

"No." Anthony walked away, back toward the fence where he felt more comfortable.

"Was it something I said?" Sean asked. Anthony could feel the eyes on the back of his neck as he walked the few feet away to get himself out of their happy little friend bubble.

"No, he's shy, skittish, and really fucking angry about something. Please, do me a favor? Just, keep trying, okay? He doesn't have any friends here, and I think he really needs one," Patrick murmured. He probably assumed only Sean could hear him, but it didn't quite work out that way.

Anthony hated that they talked about him as though he wasn't there. His parents had been doing that for years.

"He has you."

"Yeah, he has me. But I'm an old man; he needs friends his own age."

"Dude, you're thirty," Sean said with a laugh.

"Isn't that dead in your gay years? Shouldn't I have bowtie, a nice suit, and a cat, or something?"

"Or a twink."

"Shut up. Sean, why don't you hang out here with Anthony? I'm going to say hi to Sandy." Patrick wandered off before Anthony could protest.

"What would you like?" Sean asked as they made their way across the yard and stopped by the coolers. Anthony flipped open the lid and quickly inventoried the contents before putting his fingers on a Mike's Hard Lemonade. He did it instinctively because he and Chase always drank shit like that at parties. It had never been a big deal, not with his crowd. Everybody drank. But as he pulled it out of the ice, his gaze caught Patrick and Sandy talking. Tension lined Patrick's frame, and Anthony figured he was telling her about his breakup with Danielle. He didn't want to add any more to Patrick's stress, so he stretched, trying to play it off as he grabbed a Coke instead.

"No one is going to care," Sean murmured so the rest of the gathering wouldn't hear. "They're pretty laid-back about that kind of thing."

"I just don't want to cause any trouble. Plus, I don't really know anyone here, so I don't want to get messed up," Anthony admitted.

"You know me." Sean smiled around the words, and Anthony smiled back, shy for the first time in his life.

"Hey, come say hi to Sandy," Sean said when the moment had gone on a little too long. Anthony followed to where Patrick and Sandy stood near the door. She was hugging Patrick—a long, affectionate thing—and they waited for the display to be over. Then Sean tugged on Anthony's shirt to pull him near where Sandy stood, cracking open a beer. She looked up at their approach and smiled. The expression warmed something in Anthony's soul. No one had been happy to see him in a long time.

"Hey, Anthony. I'm glad you came," Sandy murmured against his temple as she hugged him close.

"Thank you for inviting me." No other words would come, so he took another drink of his pop. They stood in silence for a minute or two, the time stretching awkwardly around their little circle. Finally, a girl came by and smacked Sean on the arm.

"Hey, we're going to start up a volleyball game. Want to come and play?"

Before Anthony could protest, Sean grabbed his hand and dragged him toward a flimsy net held up by strings, their own volleyball marionette. He stood surrounded by three other people—Sean, his friend Jeff, and the girl they'd picked up somewhere near the watermelon. The other friend, Chris, stood idly by, watching Jeff when the guy wasn't looking. Anthony knew exactly how that felt. He'd watched Chase like that so many times.

"Okay, I'll take Anthony. Jeff, you take Liz, cool?"

"Yep, Liz kicks ass," Jeff said and high-fived Liz as they walked around to their side of the net.

"Got any redeeming qualities here, Anthony?" Sean asked with a laugh.

"I was all state for soccer three years in a row."

"Ah, a nimble little minx, eh? Awesome, let's do it."

Chapter Thirteen

Patrick watched Anthony and Sean play volleyball from Sandy's side where they stood by the picnic table. He hadn't let go of his bottle of water, nursing it as Sandy talked. He'd decided beer wouldn't help his head or his altercation with Bren later. Instead, he kept popping painkillers and sucking down water. Anthony spiked another ball at Jeff's feet, and Patrick laughed.

"It looks like he's adjusting," Sandy said, and Patrick took his eyes off the game.

"God, I hope so. That kid's been through a lot, and I don't think it's over yet."

"What do you mean?"

"You remember me telling you about that friend Anthony came out here to stay with. They were supposed to meet but his car broke down?"

"Yeah, you said there was something hinky about it." Sandy turned to face Patrick. "Something happened."

"Anthony gave me the address of where the guy was supposed to meet him. I knew it was in the business district, so we took a ride out there before you got there to look at the car. Sandy, it was a broken-down bookstore in the middle of nowhere. The parking lot was surrounded by a rickety iron fence. It was like rape central."

"You think this kid meant to hurt him?"

"I don't know. But he hasn't been in contact since. Not one word in two weeks. Not even an email to see if Anthony is okay."

"That's fucking weird."

"It doesn't sit right," Patrick said.

"He's got you to take care of him now." Sandy put a hand on his shoulder with a sly smile.

"That's funny. He took care of me last night after Danielle dumped me and I got wasted off my ass. Said I was chucking bottles around screaming about how I hated the place. He got me to stop and dragged that fucking air mattress downstairs."

"And where did he sleep, then?" Sandy fixed Patrick with such a hard stare that he took half a step back.

"Beside me."

"You went to bed with a seventeen-year-old boy?"

"No, I passed out on an air mattress and he crawled in with me because I was sleeping in his bed."

"Yeah, that sounds better."

"Anyway, Bren apparently called during this whole mess. He must have seen me throwing shit around even if he couldn't hear me."

"How did that go?"

"He said it was too much to ask, and to sell the shit. He doesn't fucking care anymore."

"Do you believe that?"

"It doesn't matter what I believe. I can't leave him, not in the state he's in. Maybe not ever. We're all each other has left now." Patrick sighed. He saw the signs now, clear as day. Even if Bren let him go, he'd never leave. Even if Bren snapped out of it and got better, it was just the two of them.

His Ohio vacation had officially ended.

Ferndale, Michigan, had once again become home.

ANTHONY

WHEN PATRICK DRAGGED Anthony out of the party a couple hours later, Sean extracted a promise that they'd get together soon. It warmed Patrick to see Anthony finally spending time outside the liquor store, and with people who would be good friends to him.

"I'm going to drop you off at the liquor store on my way to Bren's. Do you need to stop anywhere along the way?" Patrick pulled away from the curb in front of Sandy's house, where the party still roared in full swing.

"Do you want me to come to Bren's with you?"

"I don't think that would be a good idea. It's going to be a knock-down, drag-out fight, and you don't need to be in the middle of it." Patrick watched Anthony's changing expressions—pity, sadness, and then one he didn't really understand. In the end, Anthony just sat back against the seat and didn't say anything, but Patrick could see the argument churning just below the surface.

"Will you at least shoot me an email and let me know if he's okay?" Anthony asked, and then after a beat added, "And you're okay?"

"You guys hit it off while you were there?"

"For my part."

Patrick didn't know what to say to that. He'd figured Anthony would have come out of the experience wishing he'd never met Bren. Instead, he seemed to be concerned. He wasn't sure he knew what to think of that.

"I'll let you know."

The ride back to the liquor store passed with little discussion. Mostly Anthony watched out the window with a blank expression on his young face. Rather than trying to puzzle it out, Patrick prepared himself for the battle ahead. When he dropped the kid off at the store, he sent a text to his brother.

I'm on my way over to talk. Leave the door unlocked or I'll use the key.

For the entire ten-minute ride to the house, he received no response. He didn't really expect one, but he hated the silence anyway. The images in his head—the ones of Bren finally walking away from him, from his resentment—pushed him to the edge of tears. Then they pushed him over it.

Patrick wiped his face as he got out of the RAV4. Whatever Bren's decision, he'd fight to keep his brother. Each slab of concrete on the walk to the house reminded him of the chalk drawings he used to make there, when Bren was barely old enough to toddle all over them, making him yell. The patches of grass on either side of him brought back memories of his friends playing keep-away from Bren. The kid never got the ball, but he never got frustrated and went into the house. Now, Patrick realized, Bren had just been happy when his big brother would let him play.

God, he hated himself.

One step, then the next brought him to the top of the porch. He didn't want to check and see if the door was unlocked. He didn't want to know whether or not Bren wanted to keep him out. The anniversary of the shooting would be on them soon, and Patrick had never even stopped to consider what that would do to Bren. Deep down, sometimes he wondered if it would mean that Bren would take all those pills in his medicine cabinet and just end it.

He pulled open the screen door. It moved easily in his hands. Standing in front of it to hold it out of the way, he reached for the big oak door. The knob iced his fingers on the hot June afternoon, freezing them with Bren's indifference. Patrick took a deep breath and tightened his hold and turned his hand marginally to feel it give with no resistance.

The sob returned, but he swallowed it and opened the door.

Chapter Fourteen

Bren took another drink from the can on the kitchen table, one of the sodas Anthony had left. He'd rather have a beer. He'd rather put some fucking Jack in that Coke. He'd rather do anything than have this goddamned conversation.

But there were things that needed to be said, and Bren needed to be lucid enough to say them.

The front door opened and closed. Bren didn't look up from the can. He just waited for Patrick to find him. Kind of like when they were kids, only when he went to hide, Patrick never looked. Oh, he counted, and made Bren think that maybe this time, he'd come—but then he'd just sit and watch TV or play Nintendo while Bren stayed alone in the dark.

It didn't take long. Patrick entered the kitchen and walked to the cabinet. He pulled out a glass, got some ice, and then drew water from the tap. All the while, Bren didn't look up. He didn't want to see the permanent resentment in Patrick's eyes. Not after last night. He traced the top of the can, all the little intricacies of the pull tab. The opening slit his finger, but he didn't notice that, either. He simply kept tracing.

Patrick dropped into the seat across from him at the table. He picked the seat he'd always been in as a child, just as Bren had. A constant reminder that some things in their lives never changed, would never change. Tragedy had trapped them in that perpetual stage of adolescence forever.

"I'm sorry."

"Yeah, whatev—"

"No, Bren. I am honestly sorry."

Bren raised his head and caught Patrick's gaze. Even around the red haze of a hangover, Bren saw none of the petulance, none of the resentment that normally lived there. He saw sorrow and shame, but no anger.

"Sorry you hate me? Sorry you tried to bust up the store? Sorry you slept with Anthony? What exactly are you sorry for, Patrick?"

"I don't hate you. I've never hated you. Yes, I hated taking care of the store, but not for the reason you think. I hated it because it was *your* passion and someone took that from you."

"That isn't true."

Patrick paused and then gave a slow nod. "Okay, you're probably right about that. Sometimes I didn't want to be here, to deal with the responsibility."

"And now we're honest."

"But what I've realized is that if you woke up tomorrow and decided you wanted to take the store back, I'd still stay. You're all I have left, Bren. I'm not leaving again."

Bren rested against the back of the chair and let out a breath.

"Why did you try to bust up the store?"

This time, it was Patrick's turn to sigh. He took another long drink of the water, and Bren got the impression he chose his words carefully.

"Danielle broke up with me. I took it worse than I should have."

Bren hadn't been expecting that answer. He figured it had to be something to do with being chained to him, being chained to the store. To be honest, he still didn't discount that thought.

"Fine. What about Anthony? You fucking slept with a kid in the store, Patrick." The venom that spewed out of him shocked him with its voracity. Anger had turned into rage.

Patrick held out both hands, palms out. "I didn't touch him. I swear. I was in no shape to drive home, and he put me on his mattress. To be honest, I don't remember a lot of it. Just him reaching out, being kind."

"I turned the fucking video off when you were humping him against the wall."

"What?"

"Like a fucking dog."

"No. You're lying."

The chair clattered to the floor when Bren stood up and moved around to the other end of the long table to move the mouse on the computer. It took him just a few minutes to bring up the video. The mouse caught the brunt of his anger as he hit Play and stood back to watch his brother humping Anthony in the doorframe.

"Oh my God. Why didn't he say anything?"

"Maybe he liked it."

"Bren."

Bren shoved the chair back in the direction of the table and stalked to the refrigerator. Fuck the soda. He grabbed one of the beers off the top shelf and kept walking until he got to the couch. The house remained silent, absolutely fucking silent, as he flopped onto the cushions. He didn't care if Patrick followed him. All he could see was the way Anthony had stripped off his brother's jeans and crawled into bed with him like it was nothing.

Of course he hadn't turned the fucking camera off. He'd watched every minute of it. Anthony had to know Bren would be watching. Just showed how much the kid gave a shit about him.

"Are you angry because he's seventeen or because he's a guy?"

Bren didn't answer. His hands shook as he took another drink of the beer. Goddamn it. It was right on this couch. They'd shared, what? Sex. Pizza. A movie. Since he'd come home from the hospital two years before, it was the first time someone actually wanted to sit and spend time with him. And his brother fucking took it.

His brother took everything.

His toys.

His store.

Now Anthony.

"Go to hell, Patrick."

"What is your fucking problem, Bren?" Patrick dropped onto the love seat. "I don't get it. I didn't touch Anthony like that. He put my drunk ass on that stupid mattress and slept there because he had no other options. Why is this such an issue for you? It's not like I stole your...." Patrick's eyes widened, and he sat up perfectly straight as Bren slumped farther down the couch.

"Fuck you."

"How is that even possible? You guys were only here for an hour or—"

"He came back."

"What do you mean he came back?"

"He took the bus and came back, a couple times now. I told him I liked movies but couldn't do the violence anymore. He brought over *Harry Potter*. We order pizza and hang out. I think we just finished the third one."

"Oh."

"He emails too."

"Oh. Oh no."

"Oh no, what?" Bren tossed the empty bottle somewhere in the direction of the table. It banged off the side and landed on the carpet.

"I didn't know, Bren. I swear I didn't. I just... I hooked him up with Sean. I wanted him to have friends here, maybe even a summer fling."

"Of course you did." Bren scoffed. "Whatever. He's probably better off with metrosexual Sean than the angry, broken drunk anyway."

"I don't think—"

"Just go, Patrick. I don't need anyone else to resent me."

Chapter Fifteen

"Are you sure you want to give these to me?" Anthony stared wide-eyed at the key in his hand. It sat atop a piece of paper with a four-digit code. He didn't even have a key to his parents' house because someone was always home, and of course his parents wanted to keep track of his movements. That was why he'd just started crawling in and out of the window.

Patrick grinned. "I told you I'd give you one after your probation was over. You've earned it. Plus, I have a feeling you're going to be out late tonight, so you'll need it. Where are you guys headed?"

"I don't know." Anthony couldn't tear his eyes away from the key and everything it symbolized. "Sean said something about a beach." He looked up at Patrick. "Are we near the water?"

"Have you not looked at a map?" Patrick asked with a laugh. "We're right on Lake Huron. Didn't you notice that you passed a lake to get here?"

"I didn't, actually. I just kind of followed the directions. It never occurred to me to find out what might be there." Anthony closed his eyes for a second and then opened them again slowly. "Jesus, I'm an idiot. I never even thought about what I was doing before I left. Not once."

"It's called learning from your mistakes, kiddo. We all do it. Some lessons are just harder than others. He's probably taking you over to Metropark. They spend a lot of time hanging out there."

"Yeah, that was it. Is there anything special I need to know?"

"Nope, they're good guys. Take a sweatshirt. It gets cold on the lakefront at night."

"Thanks."

The bell sounded on the front door, and they both glanced up to see Sean come in with Jeff and Chris tagging behind. Chris wandered off down the aisle of mixes, and Jeff went over for beer. Sean bumped Anthony's arm with his own. Anthony liked the casual mix of board shorts, Keds, and neatly preppy pastel T-shirt he wore. It was nothing Anthony could have pulled off, but he liked the way Sean did.

"Hey, I love that T-shirt." Sean pulled the hem of it away from Anthony's skin. "Outbreak Monkey is one of my favorite bands."

"Me too. I like what they've been doing since Mackey got out of rehab."

"His stuff was always intense."

"Yeah."

They stood around in awkward silence as Patrick sat behind the register and counted down the day drawer. Kevin had already started stocking the weird cooler, the stuff with wine coolers and imports. Anthony got the impression he just ticked down the minutes until his boss got the hell out of his way.

"Okay, I'm going to run up and get a hoodie. I'll be back in a minute," Anthony said to escape the fucked-up new-friend silence. That way, they could talk about him. He took more time than he needed because he also checked his email quickly. Nothing from Jay, nothing from his parents, but always something from Bren.

It's been a bad day. Want to come over tonight and watch a movie?

Oh damn. Now he wished he hadn't made plans with Sean. It was the first time Bren had ever asked him to come over. Usually he made innuendos or sometimes forwarded links to YouTube videos he liked, never once had he said "come on over." With that, Anthony had two choices. He could pretend he hadn't gotten the email until tomorrow when it would be too late, or he could find his balls and answer it.

He closed the laptop and grabbed the hoodie before he could change his mind.

"So, there's not much around here. The college is pretty small. But we go out to the beach and just hang out. Sometimes we play beach volleyball if it's not too crowded. Usually, there's not a lot of people there after dark. But we have a place that's pretty remote, so we can do... you know, whatever."

Sean winked at Anthony, who sat in the front seat of the truck next to him while Jeff and Chris took the back. Anthony didn't turn around to look, but from the sounds and movements he could see out of the corner of his eye, it seemed as though they were getting kind of handsy back there.

Anthony saw a sign for Metropark, but they kept driving a mile or so down the road until they came to a barely-there opening in the trees. Sean parked the truck behind a small cluster and they got out.

"There's a trail here that leads to the beach," Sean explained. "This way we don't have to worry about pesky things like when the park closes." He laughed and led the way through the trees. Every sound in the brush startled Anthony. He'd seen too many fucking horror movies to be able to make it through peacefully. Any moment, Jason would come out of the lake and murder him with the dull end of an oar. Then, after a new more steps, Michael lurked from behind that goddamned fallen tree off to the right, and he'd have a machete the size of a car. He jumped when Sean put a hand on his shoulder.

"You okay?"

"Yeah. Where I'm from, a walk in the woods usually ends up with you on the news," Anthony admitted, and Sean laughed.

"Same here, most of the time. But we aren't lost in the woods. We're moving with purpose." Sean held his hand out, and Anthony saw a clearing ahead. *Oh, thank fuck.* The trail changed from dirt-packed leaves and mulchy twigs to sand, and they trudged through it on their way to the open water. Dark and sparkling, the lake went on for miles, overtaking the world before them.

"The fire pit is over here," Jeff said. "Let's grab some branches and wood from the trees to burn."

He and Chris started the hunt, and Anthony joined in, foraging at the edge of the woods, picking up pieces and discarding anything wet or covered in ick. He had no idea, really, what he was looking for. They'd never built fires at home. At least, not on purpose.

"That's good," Chris finally announced, and they carried bushels of pieces in their arms about thirty feet onto the beach where a circle of rocks and a few fallen logs waited for them. Footprints and assorted left-behind odds and ends—a flip-flop here, a hoodie there—littered the area around the logs.

They dropped the wood into the pit, and Chris started to arrange it into some meaningful order, at least meaningful to him. Anthony stood off to the side, watching the waves as they crashed into the shoreline. For the first time since he'd landed in Patrick's lap, he felt peace.

"It's kind of overwhelming, huh?" Sean asked from his shoulder as another wave made its way onto the sand.

"The lake? It's the only thing in my life that isn't overwhelming right now. In fact, it's pretty calming here."

"You did just run away from home. I guess that's enough to set anyone's life spinning."

He didn't ask why Anthony left; he didn't push. Anthony appreciated that. He spent another minute watching the water, taking in the serenity of it, and then went back to the circle, where Chris had the branches starting to burn.

"Anthony, welcome to Detroit," Jeff said and handed him a beer out of the cooler they'd lugged from the truck. He popped the top and took a pull. For a long moment, he tried to remember if he'd ever had a drink just for the sheer enjoyment of it. In the years since he'd started, he'd only ever used the alcohol to block out the unpleasantness of his life.

"Are you guys from Detroit?" he asked, just to have something to talk about.

"I'm from Ferndale," Jeff said. "It's like I'm trapped here by some kind of quantum tunneling effect."

"I'm from Lansing, but my parents moved here because my dad's job changed about five years ago," Chris said.

"I'm from Parma, Michigan. It's about a hundred miles west," Sean offered. "I moved here when I started college."

"Wait, you're from Parma?" Jeff asked, a quirk at the corner of his mouth.

Chris smiled too.

"I don't understand, what's wrong with Parma?" Anthony asked.

"That makes him... Parma Sean." Chris said, causing Jeff to snort beer out of his nose.

"This is why I'm looking for different friends," Sean confided to Anthony, who laughed.

"Thank you for inviting me out," Anthony told Sean. Then to try to match the joking tenor of the moment, he added, "I can only read and surf Internet porn so much." He thought it would make them laugh, but the guys just nodded.

"You a Tube8 man, or XTube?" Jeff asked, and Anthony choked on his beer.

"Uhm, I was kidding. I'm... I...." Anthony sputtered and Jeff laughed.

"I know, I just wanted to see how far you'd take it."

"I'm a Tube8 man myself," Chris said, ignoring the banter. "It's not just thirty-second promos for shit you have to pay for."

"Right?" Sean piped in. "If I'm gonna go get my rocks off, I don't want to keep taking my hand off my dick to find another video."

Anthony's face burned. He'd never heard anyone, not even Chase, talk so brazenly about sex or porn.

"Anthony, you're so red that you're glowing," Jeff said and put a hand on his arm.

"I just... I've never really talked about stuff like this before. I didn't know anyone besides my brother who was gay. And he never talked about sex. It freaked him out."

"Sex freaked him out?"

"Yeah, he'd been assaulted. It bothered him to think about it."

"Damn, I don't know what I'd do if I couldn't fuck or at least rub one out," Chris admitted. "If I could major in it at college, I'd graduate on the dean's list."

"Not even that could get you on the dean's list. Been there, done that," Jeff said and Sean laughed.

"Damn, burn!"

Chris glowered in Jeff's direction. "Says the guy who was bouncing on my dick last night."

"Oh my God," Anthony whispered to no one. He wanted to laugh. He wanted to giggle like a teenage girl, but that seemed kind of uncool, so he kept it inside.

"Anyway," Sean said. "What's going on with you, Anthony? Patrick said you and Bren got to be friends. Way to go there. No one has penetrated his armor in a long time."

"He-he, you said 'penetrated,'" Jeff muttered, and the circle started laughing again.

"You're an idiot." Chris leaned over and biffed him on the head.

"I don't know," Anthony said, trying to ignore their laughter but failing as he chuckled through his explanation. "Sometimes he'd a dick, sometimes he's fun. He just looked like he could use a friend, and I sure as hell could. And... uhm... he gives good head."

"Wait, what?" Sean bellowed so loudly that a small contingent of birds escaped from the trees into the air.

"No way!" Jeff said, and suddenly all eyes were on Anthony as they waited for his explanation.

"Bren's gay?" Sean's eyes were wide.

"Patrick had me go over there to help Bren with a repair guy, and we got bored. He said we should fuck, but the guy got there, so we just did oral. Which was okay because I wasn't sure I wanted to do that." Anthony looked away toward the lake again, wishing that its cool watery depths would stop the burning in his cheeks.

"Why weren't you sure?" Sean asked, his voice gentle.

"I haven't done that before," Anthony admitted. He started to stand so he could walk to the water's edge and escape the conversation, but Sean grabbed his arm.

"Hey man, there's nothing wrong with that. We're not going to razz you about it."

"I just feel stupid."

"Hey, it's like douching, man, just let it all out," Jeff said, and the other two guys groaned.

"I can't believe you just said that."

"I...." Anthony started but lost his nerve, all bravado melting onto the sand in the heat of the fire.

"You... what?" Sean asked.

He stared into the fire, anything to avoid the eyes on him.

"I don't know what douching means."

"Oh!" Sean said with a quiet laugh. "That just means cleaning things out if you bottom."

"How do you...?"

"Depends on the guy, and what you have handy," Chris supplied. "Some guys use an actual enema kit without the medication stuff. Some guys use a squirt bottle like those old-fashioned ketchup bottles—"

"Oh, ew," Sean said. "I just use a water bottle, like a Dasani bottle."

"A water bottle?"

"A water bottle. Get in the shower, turn on the warm water, fill up the bottle, and shoot it a few times. When the water's clean, it's ready for peen."

"Wow."

"Really?"

"Okay, I think that calls for another beer." Anthony stood up and walked over to the cooler, his mind reeling. He grabbed four bottles and distributed them even though his still sat half full in the sand. The break helped him to process things, and he sat back on the log.

"So, how do you know who is going to, well...?" Anthony swallowed and pulled on his big-boy pants. "Who is going to fuck and who gets fucked?"

"That's all what you like, usually. See, Jeff here is a big ol' bottom. He'd rather get fucked than fuck. I'm a top. I'd rather do the fucking. Chris is pretty versatile. He doesn't care as long as he's getting some. You don't really know until you try it."

"Wanna try it?" Chris asked with a wink.

"Out here in the sand? No thanks," Anthony said as his dick hardened against his jeans. He didn't want to admit it, but the refusal had more to do with fear than sand. He didn't know Chris, really, not beyond their superficial conversations. For letting someone into his body, he wanted a little more trust than small talk.

"Well, if you're interested, you have my number."

"I'm interested," Jeff piped up.

"Yeah?" Chris stood up and held a hand out to Jeff. Anthony watched in disbelief as they headed back toward the woods in the direction they'd come.

"Got a water bottle?" Sean called after them, and Anthony put his head in his hands.

"They're really going to go out there and fuck?"

"Yeah, it happens."

The two of them stayed quiet for a long while, watching the waves or the dancing flames. Every once in a while, Anthony thought he heard the sound of slapping skin, but it could have been the waves. Once or twice he heard a moan that he wrote off as the wind. He'd nearly decided to walk back to the liquor store, when something occurred to him.

"Hey, you've known Bren and Patrick for a while, right?" he asked, turning on the log to face Sean.

"Yeah, I worked there for about three years, why?"

"What was Bren like before?"

"Before the shooting, you mean?"

"Yeah."

"I don't know. He was the all-around jock. He played football. He liked cars. He was a couple years ahead of me in school, and I remember him being popular but kind. Bren wasn't the kind of guy to let his football buddies fuck with someone. He's just push them and tell them to move along. I always liked that about him, being the quiet gay kid."

"Was he out?"

"I didn't know he was gay until you said you'd fucked around with him."

"Did he have girlfriends?" Anthony watched the water, wanting to know, but not wanting to know about Bren's teenaged love life.

"I don't know. I was a freshman and he was a senior. It seemed like he did, but then all the guys on the team did. He was outgoing, always making jokes. Everyone liked him. Then after, when he came home from the hospital, no one knew what to say or how to help him. He was angry all the time and wouldn't come out of the house. After a while, people just stopped trying."

"Yeah, my brother was the same way. I remembered his friends at the house all the time before, and then after, they just stopped coming because he wouldn't see them."

"I'd have to guess it's hard to adjust when your life changes like that. I'm lucky, I've never had something horrible happen."

"I've never had it happen to me, but what happened to my brother was like an eclipse over our family."

"It must suck to never see the sun," Sean said.

"I see it now."

Chapter Sixteen

"Dude, he's going to be here soon. Are you fucking ready yet?" Bren asked for the third time as Patrick pulled another container of wings out of the bag. He set them on the counter with a pan of baked macaroni and cheese Butch had made for the occasion. Sandy had added a couple of two liters of soda.

"Yes, Jesus, calm down. It's not a wedding, man," Patrick tossed over his shoulder as he arranged the wings in the warming tin and moved it to the end of the counter to start the buffet line. Bren dropped paper plates, napkins, and plastic forks that the three amigos had brought. He hated that that little fuck Sean and Anthony had ignored him when he asked for help. Wasn't that what he was he supposed to do, ask for help? What was the point if no one answered?

"What about the cake?"

"I put it in the refrigerator when I got here." Patrick surveyed the counter. "Which was an impressive feat given the amount of beer in there."

"The fact that it's still in there should make you happy."

"It does." Patrick turned toward his brother. He didn't hug Bren, which was fine, but he had that sappy "I'm so glad you're my brother" look. Bren rolled his eyes and went into the living room.

"Maybe the bus is—"

"He's coming up the street," Bren said. Sandy and Butch grabbed Sean, and they all went into the kitchen to hide. Surprises weren't a bright spot in Bren's day, but something in his soul wanted to make it special for Anthony. Fucking Sean. Bren wanted so much more than just one special moment.

Thirty seconds... a minute... ninety seconds... and a knock at the door. He turned to make sure Anthony wouldn't be able to see anyone from the door and then turned the handle.

"Hey," he said, stepping back to let Anthony inside.

"It's a bitch of a day out there. I think I just sweated my balls off," Anthony commented as he stepped inside. "Thank God that guy fixed the air. Though his timing couldn't have been—"

"Hey, I got wings instead of pizza. Are you hungry?" Bren asked, effectively cutting off whatever Anthony would add to the end of that sentence. He didn't need their sexual escapades announced to the whole fucking world.

"Yeah, I love wings."

"Cool, go ahead into the kitchen and make a plate. I'll throw the movie in. I picked up *Fantastic Four*. It should be fine. No gun violence, just guys beating the crap out of each other." Bren waited until Anthony started for the kitchen and then followed as quietly as he could.

"That's cool, I'd been wanting to see—"

"*Surprise!*"

The kitchen exploded with laughter and chatter. Bren wanted to take a picture of Anthony's face in that moment, full of wonder and emotion. Patrick hugged him, and then Sandy hugged him. Bren had been about to come in and put a hand on Anthony's shoulder when he bolted from the room past him, pushing his way away from the crowd around the cake.

Bren stared at Patrick, who stared right back.

Well, no one really expected Anthony to run out of the room.

Chaos theory at its finest.

Bren left Patrick to deal with the confused partygoers, and he followed Anthony to the bedroom. Listening at the door, he didn't hear anything, so he knocked. It took a few seconds for the doorknob to turn. When it opened, Bren's heart broke. Which surprised him, since he didn't think he actually had one left. Anthony's eyes were bright and wet, his face flushed. Bren watched him for half a second before he came into the room, and Anthony bridged the gap to step into his arms.

"What is it?" Bren whispered into Anthony's hair, running his fingers through the overgrown mess. God, they both needed haircuts. Too bad neither of them cared.

"I feel so stupid," Anthony said, his voice drifting toward laughter.

"Why?"

"No one has ever thrown a party for me before. I mean, I probably had birthday parties as a kid, but parents kind of have to do that. I can't believe you guys did this."

"Patrick saw your birthday on your paperwork. He wanted you to spend the day with people who care about you."

Anthony nodded. It seemed he was beyond words.

"Let's hang out here for a minute, and then we can go back out. There's cake. And beer."

Anthony laughed through his tears.

"There's always beer."

"Thank Christ for that."

It took a minute for Anthony to get himself together enough for them to rejoin the party. No one said anything to him about his little emotional meltdown. Patrick met Bren's eyes over Anthony's head, and his expression told Bren they'd be having a chat later.

They laughed and talked around the food, picking through the wings, as they sat in chairs and leaned against counters. Not once since the funeral had Bren had so many people in his house. If he were completely honest with himself, he'd admit he didn't mind so much. But Bren had never been completely honest with himself. He didn't much like where honesty got him.

Well, okay, he kind of wished them all gone when they started singing. Bren cringed and Anthony did the awkward moment of silence while he waited for them to finish their birthday rendition, so off-key it was in a completely different universe of bad. Then he puckered his lips, and Bren's cock twinged while Anthony blew out the candles. He had something Anthony could blow after everyone else left.

Bren felt pretty good, he had to admit. His life had its good days and bad. Mostly bad.

But today was a good day.

He glanced around the kitchen, peeking around the refrigerator, but didn't see Anthony. Frowning, Bren checked around the corner into the living room and wished he hadn't. Anthony stood there with Sean, a fork against his lips as Sean fed him cake off his own plate. He laughed at something Sean said and frosting spilled from the corner of his mouth, and Sean wiped it away with his thumb. The scene, so intimate, froze Bren's blood.

Without a word, he grabbed a six-pack, walked into his bedroom and slammed the door.

Fuck. Them. All.

The knock on his bedroom door woke him out of an alcohol-induced sleep. Everything remained hazy around the edges, blurring and fogging like a windshield on a cold, rainy day. It took a minute for him to register Anthony standing just inside the door, cowering maybe, but there nonetheless.

"I thought you'd be off fucking Sean," Bren said, his manners giving way to the hostile greeting. Trust wasn't something he gave easily, and the fucking kid snuck in and took it anyway.

"What?"

"You guys were all cozy earlier. I assumed you'd be off with him."

"Is that why you've been holed up in here? You think I'm fucking Sean?" The rage in Anthony's eyes burned clear through to flush his cheeks. They took on a red hue, boiling steam, raging fires, all contained beneath the surface of his skin.

Bren didn't answer right away. He rolled over onto his back, searching for an exit to make the room stop spinning. He didn't fucking need this. Goddamn it, he might not have been happy before this kid weaseled his way into his life, but he knew what to expect. He knew he'd get up in the morning, or sometimes in the afternoon. He knew he'd eat. He knew he'd drink. He knew he'd pass out. Now he felt as though he'd fallen into the spin cycle on his fucking washing machine.

"No, I think Sean is fucking you," Bren spat and threw his legs over the side of the bed. He still had his jeans on, but he picked up his shirt off the floor.

Anthony didn't move. He didn't speak. He didn't make eye contact with Bren. The only indication he'd even heard Bren's accusation stayed clenched in Anthony's fists on either side of his body. Bren knew the rise and fall of Anthony's chest, slow, steady, controlled, meant he was working to control his temper. Bren didn't want him to control his temper. He wanted to fight, to get it all out, to punch something.

Anthony wouldn't give him that, which pissed him off even more.

"Fuck. You."

Without another word, Anthony turned and headed for the bedroom door, and maybe out of Bren's life. The idea of never seeing Anthony again tore at something inside him that he didn't think would heal. The rage boiled over his ability to contain it.

"Don't come back." The words were meant to come out as a growl, but it turned into a scream. His voice cracked in the middle on the strength of a sob. Anthony paused, almost as if he wanted to answer, but then kept walking, out of the bedroom, out of the house, and out of his life.

Bren closed his eyes and waited for the pain to break him.

Chapter Seventeen

Jesus, why did life have to be so fucking hard? Anthony understood now why that seemed to be Aaron's personal motto. Just when he thought maybe he'd found something good, fate snatched it from him. He wished he could just catch a break.

The walk from the bus took him right next to the pizza place, so he stopped for dinner before wandering back to the liquor store. Kevin waved as Anthony made his way to the pint room and the stairs that led to his tiny, rundown apartment. Even it had started to feel claustrophobic in the wake of Bren's accusations. If they didn't want him there anymore, maybe he could talk to Sean about somewhere else. He only needed a couple more weeks to finish saving for the car. He could couch-surf until then, right?

Anthony dropped the pizza on the empty table and grabbed his laptop from the bed. Maybe he could find something online in a Craigslist ad. He just hoped Patrick would let him keep the job until he found something else.

His third pizza that week helped to fill the hole inside him as he looked through the ads. Most of the rents were more than he made in a month. He'd have to give up food and his car to move out of the apartment over the store. He found one that maybe he could do, a room for rent. He clicked on the link to respond by email and fired off a request for information. He was about to close his inbox when he saw he had new email.

It wasn't from Bren.

His heart raced as he double-clicked on the subject line, which read: *I'm so sorry.*

Anthony,

My dad found out that you were coming and stopped me from meeting you. He was so angry that he put me on lockdown. He wouldn't let me write or call. I finally convinced him to let me email you to see if you're okay. I saw your email that said that you're staying with someone in Ferndale. Are you okay there? My dad's not mad anymore and says you can come stay with us. We can even come get you.

I miss you,

Jay

Anthony blinked and read it again. And again. He read it until it blurred through his tears. He read it until the ball of flame in his throat threatened to consume him. Then he read it again and put the laptop in his lap, fingers on the keys. Instead of emailing, he switched to chat.

I could have been dead.

His chat dinged, reminding him that by logging into chat, he was visible to the world. Fuck the world. He took his status to offline and opened the chat window to read Jay's message.

I know you're angry. I didn't know what to do.

I'm sorry.

Please.

Anthony looked away, over the cooling pizza and out of the small window above his makeshift bed. God, he wanted to believe Jay. He wanted someone to still want him to be there, to want him to be fucking anywhere. No one had posted on his wall. No one had emailed but Allen. Now Bren had pushed Anthony out of his life. It wouldn't be too long before Patrick did the same, and then he'd be alone again.

Why should I trust you?

You said I could come and stay with you and then you disappeared.

He waited because the response seemed to take longer that time. Maybe Jay had to think of another lie to tell. Maybe he was trying to decide how to earn back Anthony's trust.

I guess you have no reason to trust me.

I wish I could see you. You're so close.
I've missed you so much.
Something inside of Anthony tore at that. He missed Jay too. Whenever life seemed too hard, Jay had always made it better. God, he didn't know what to do.
I miss you too.
The ding again, and Anthony forced himself to look at the screen.
Please, just let me and my dad come get you. If you don't like it here, we can take you back.
I just really want to see you.
Anthony took a long, slow, deep breath. He wanted to think he'd learned from his mistakes. Just over a month ago, he'd packed up everything he owned and left on the word of someone who then abandoned him. If it weren't for Patrick and Bren, he'd have nothing.
I will meet you. That's all I can promise for now.
He closed the box of pizza as his stomach churned around the anxiety inside it.
Where?
Where indeed. Jay didn't need to be inside the liquor store. Anthony was only inside because he worked there. Maybe the pizza place. No, he didn't want anywhere associated with him in case things went bad. Jay didn't know where he was. He only knew it was a liquor store. Until he could trust Jay, maybe they should keep things on neutral ground. But it had to be someplace close enough so he could run.
The Sunoco on Woodward Ave and Ardmore Dr.
The box dinged again almost immediately.
We can be there tonight around eight?
Eight would make it nearly dark, but the gas station was always pretty well lit.
Fine.
The final message came through as clear as a bell.

I can't wait to see you.

Anthony slammed his laptop closed and grabbed the pizza. He'd lost his appetite. Between the fight with Bren and Jay's sudden reappearance into his life, he didn't want to think about food or anything else right then. Several minutes passed as he stood at the top of the stairs, pizza in one hand, railing in the other. Then he moved, the world starting to spin again.

"Hey, Anthony, can we talk for a minute?" Patrick called from the front as Anthony snuck into the cooler to throw his pizza next to the partial gallon of milk and six-pack of Pepsi he'd left there.

His day had just gone from bad to worse.

"Yeah," Anthony called, coming up the middle aisle between the different styles of wine. The whites, the reds, the sparkling, they all mocked him as he passed. Each shiny bottle poised for sale, perfectly attuned to its place in the world.

Patrick asked Kevin to take over up front and then jerked his head toward the front door.

"Let's take a walk."

Anthony wondered if that was some kind of boss code for "you're fired" but followed anyway. Once they passed the edge of the parking lot, they turned left toward the busier part of town.

"You hungry?" Patrick asked as Anthony recognized the path to the pizza place.

"No, I just threw a mostly uneaten pizza in the cooler." He caught the expression of surprise on Patrick's face, so like Bren's, it hurt to look at.

"Okay, let's just sit and have a Coke, then. Is that cool?"

He walked beside Patrick until they reached the pizza place, which seemed to be pretty dead, even for a Monday. Instead of going up to the counter, he grabbed a booth in the back while Patrick got their drinks. If the man was going to fire him, the least he could do was pay for the fucking pop.

ANTHONY

Two minutes passed, and then five while Anthony sat waiting for the future to close in around him. The room seemed to be doing a brilliant job of that all on its own. It felt confining and dark, even though it looked the same as every other time he'd been in there.

Patrick came back with two cups, a slice balanced on one of them. After setting his haul on the table, he dropped down into the booth across from Anthony and sighed.

"If you're going to fire me, just do it already." Anthony's patience snapped against the strain of the day. He grabbed the straw and slammed it against the table to pop open the paper, bending it to fuck in the process.

"What? Why would I fire you?" Patrick's face paled as he looked at Anthony with wide, shocked eyes. Whatever the conversation would be about, apparently that wasn't it.

"For pissing off your brother. Isn't it his store?"

"My brother is always pissed off. Of course I'm not going to fire you."

"I figured you'd want me gone. He certainly does."

"Even if he did, it's not like I'd let you just leave with nowhere else to go."

"I have somewhere else to go." Anthony leaned against the back of the booth and leveled Patrick an even stare.

"What do you mean?"

"I heard from Jay today. He and his dad are coming to meet me tonight." Anthony shrugged and took a drink from his cup. Patrick sat completely still. Not even his eyelids moved as the shock in his face moved to anger.

"So, he just called you out of the blue?"

"Emailed, actually."

"Are you out of your fucking mind?" Patrick glanced around and nodded apologetically at the older couple seated a few booths down as they tsked at him.

"Your brother doesn't want me. Sean doesn't want me. Maybe Jay does. I'm fucking sick of being unwanted."

"Do you hear yourself? You sound like a child, Anthony. You're not just going to sell yourself off to the highest bidder, hoping that someone pats you on the head." Patrick threw his hands up in frustration.

"Fuck you, Patrick."

"Where are you meeting him?"

"None of your—"

"Where?" Patrick growled, and Anthony didn't think he'd ever seen Patrick so angry, not even the night he'd busted up the store.

"They're meeting me at the Sunoco across the street."

"When?"

Anthony sighed. He didn't really have any reason not to tell Patrick except pure stubbornness. Besides, he'd only recently been given a key to the store. If the thing with Jay fell through, he didn't want to have to go back to having a curfew.

"Eight."

"I'll be there."

"What?"

"If you're going, I'm going. I'm not going to let you go alone to meet the creepy fucking stranger that wanted to drag you out behind that bookstore and do God knows what to you."

"I can take care of myself."

"I know that. I've seen that since you've been here. You're incredibly resilient. But what I'm telling you, Anthony, is that you don't have to do everything alone."

Anthony's chest tightened, as if something inside of him grew too big to fit. It burned, and he closed his eyes against the weight of it. He'd only ever relied on Allen, and Allen had left. Now he was starting to rely on Patrick and Bren.

Bren.

Goddamn it.

"Fine."

They sat across from each other in the booth. Awkward silence built between them, clogging the air, swirling with the smell of garlic and the sounds of clashing pans until Anthony couldn't stand it.

"You said you wanted to talk to me about something?" he prompted.

Patrick shook his head. "After that, I'd almost forgotten. I wanted to talk to you about Bren."

"Not a chance." Anthony slid to his right. His ass had just hit the edge of the booth when Patrick put a hand on his to stop him.

"Please."

The expression Patrick wore, open and pleading, pushed him back into the booth. He'd just promised to be there for Anthony later that evening when he met Jay. Maybe to protect him, maybe just for support, but Anthony owed it to Patrick to listen.

"I don't know what there is to say. He thinks I'm sleeping with Sean. I don't know why he even cares. It's not like he wants to, you know, get together."

"You need to understand," Patrick started. He glanced out the window beside them, as though maybe he was trying to find the words. "Bren was a different person before the shooting. There wasn't anything he couldn't do. School, sports, friends—I envied him, to be honest. Nothing ever came that easy to me. I always wanted him to do something amazing with his life, not just run a liquor store. But in a horribly selfish way, I'm glad he wanted to do it, because I never did. I guess this is karma's way of biting me in the ass."

"Sean told me some about what Bren was like. But it doesn't matter what he *was* like, Patrick. I never knew that Bren."

"He's abrasive and angry, totally self-contained inside that house and his head. I don't know what to do for him." Patrick leaned forward, his expression earnest. "But he's been different since you showed up. Not like he wants to try to live again, but maybe like he'd consider trying. If that makes any sense."

"Yeah, I lived with Aaron for almost a decade. It took a long time for him to want to leave the house. I don't know what made him go to college, but that's where he met Spencer and it helped. Not falling in love with Spencer, but getting out of the house, meeting his therapist, and figuring out that there's a world outside our front door. I guess I just figured that out too."

"A world with Sean?" Patrick probed.

"Sean and I aren't together. He wanted to fuck at the beach; I said no. I didn't want that. Not with him." Anthony glanced out the window.

"Really?"

"Yeah. I just didn't want to."

"Because of Bren?"

"Fuck if I know."

"Anthony, no matter how you feel about Bren, at least be his friend. He really needs that right now whether he wants it or not."

Anthony huffed out a breath. "I don't know what I want, to be honest. I've never had choices like this before. It's always been whatever was best for Aaron, that's what my family did. I know I want to meet Jay. I know I want to keep working for you. I know I want you and Bren in my life. Beyond that, I have no idea what's going to happen."

"Me either, Anthony, but if you want, we can figure it out together."

"Because I remind you of your brother."

"No, actually. Not anymore. You and I have more in common than you and he have. Life has done its best to kick your ass, and you're not only standing, you're stronger. That's what I want for Bren."

Anthony had no idea what to say to that, so he didn't say anything.

He just waited for the storm.

Chapter Eighteen

The clock in Patrick's head banged with each tick as he waited for the storm. He didn't know what would happen when Anthony came down from the apartment to meet this "Jay." He didn't know how he would face his brother if he let Anthony leave with a stranger.

Most of all, he didn't know how to make any of it stop.

"Are you going to hang around here all day?" Kevin asked as he filled open spots in the pints on the shelf behind the register. Two Smirnoff, a couple of Crowns, and one Grey Goose they hadn't had to restock in a while.

"I have some paperwork to do. Got a problem?"

"Other than the fact that you're not actually doing paperwork? Nope."

Patrick pulled a stack of invoices toward him, rattling them so Kevin would see, and then stared right past them. He'd pay them. Maybe not right then, but eventually. He flipped the pages again and wondered why he gave a shit what Kevin thought. He'd never really liked the man. His father hadn't, either. But he showed up on time, had little ambition to change jobs, and didn't bitch too much. The perfect employee.

"Hey kid, it's gonna storm later. Be careful," Kevin called out, and Patrick glanced up to see Anthony walking to the front doors.

"Thanks, Kevin. I'll be back in a bit."

Patrick half stood up, his knees slamming on the fucking keyboard drawer he kept meaning to take out. It took a second, but he slumped back into his chair. If Anthony wanted his company, he'd have asked, and now Patrick had bruises.

After an hour of Kevin's sideways glances, he'd had enough. He still had an hour and a half before this stupid meeting took place. His bones ached with the anticipation of it, and he couldn't keep his body in the chair. Though he didn't think he'd have much of an appetite, Patrick headed out of the office with a wave at Kevin. He hit the sidewalk and went right, where his favorite sushi place happened to be.

He'd just pulled the handle on the door when he saw Anthony turn the corner and head up the block toward him. He seemed to be in his own world, staring at the sidewalk before his feet. Patrick ducked into the restaurant and watched him pass. Nothing fazed him—not the bird that swooped over his head or the shriek of a car horn as it passed.

"Just one, Mr. Patrick?"

"Just one today," Patrick told the kind older hostess who sat him almost every time he frequented the place. She led him to a table in front of a window near the front door. Patrick looked out toward the sidewalk, but Anthony had gone. For a moment, he wondered if the boy had wandered back up to the apartment, but then the waitress came and offered him green tea.

He didn't need a menu. A creature of habit, he always ordered edamame to hold him over until his spider roll arrived. That visit was no exception, and he munched mindlessly on the beans while he stared out the window.

A shadow passed over his face, and he glanced up just as Anthony passed by the window again. He wore the same grim expression, still pointed toward the sidewalk. The kid must have been walking aimlessly around the block trying to work something out. He considered having Anthony come inside and talk about it, but some things you just had to figure out for yourself. Besides, they'd already talked about it.

His phone buzzed as he unwrapped the chopsticks.

Why is he walking circles around the block?

Patrick should have known Bren would be watching. He was always watching.

He's thinking.

The waitress arrived with his roll, and he picked up the first piece as his phone buzzed again. He popped the sushi in his mouth and took a minute before checking his text.

About what?

He didn't want to tell Bren about Anthony's meeting later with this "Jay." As the previous few weeks had proven, stress wasn't something his brother dealt with well, especially when he could do nothing about it. Helplessness seemed to be Bren's constant companion, and Patrick refused to add to it.

You.

At least that was partly the truth.

Me?

Oh for the love of God.

He likes you Bren. Not just as a buddy to watch movies with. You have to know this. But you took his fucking head off for no reason. He isn't sleeping with Sean. He told Sean no, and I'm pretty sure it was because of you.

The phone stayed silent for a while, long enough for Patrick to eat two more pieces of his roll. Then he took a drink of his tea. And still, he waited.

Finally, his phone buzzed again.

What am I supposed to do with that?

Well, at least it wasn't a flat-out denial. That meant something.

I know you care about him. Tell him that.

He didn't get another text after that, and he didn't expect to. Bren had always been one to work things out on his own. Lately, he needed a general push in the right direction, but aside from his trauma issues, he usually found his way. Patrick hoped he would with Anthony too.

Speaking of Anthony, he was passing by the window yet again, and Patrick glanced at his watch. Seven thirty. He called for the check and watched out the window while he waited. Anthony had given up the chase around the block and simply stood in front of the liquor store, off to the side of the windows, where Kevin wouldn't see him. He stared across the street at the gas station, and Patrick wondered if Anthony saw the same threats in the shadows that Patrick saw.

He left cash on the table and headed out. Anthony didn't look away from the Sunoco but half-smiled anyway.

"I thought you'd given up the ghost and gone home."

"Not a chance."

"Whatever happens, thank you."

Patrick didn't want to consider the "whatever happens" part of the equation. He wouldn't let Anthony go with them, he knew that. It was just a matter of figuring out how to get him to stop.

"I heard from Bren."

"Yeah?" Anthony turned for the first time and drew his gaze away from the gas station. He watched Patrick, apprehension clear in his eyes.

"He wanted to know why you were walking around in circles."

"Fuck, I forgot about the stupid cameras. Did you tell him about tonight?"

"No, I told him you were thinking about him."

"That's not a lie."

"I know."

They both stared across the street, waiting in the calm before the storm. Patrick had no idea what thoughts ran through Anthony's head. Anticipation, fear, longing—nothing showed in his expression. It appeared oddly blank.

Patrick checked the time on his phone.

Ten minutes.

ANTHONY

"Do you want to head over there? Maybe wander through the junk food while we wait?" Patrick asked, bumping Anthony's arm with his own. Anthony took a long, slow, deep breath and stopped a beat before answering.

"I'm not hungry, not in the least. I still have an entire pizza waiting in the cooler, but anything beats standing here watching the fucking traffic."

They strode side by side past the little sushi place and to the corner. Patrick jammed his finger against the button that would change the Walk sign, and they waited in silence. Nothing more needed to be said. Nothing would dissuade Anthony. All Patrick could do was watch and hope.

The sign changed, and they made their way to the opposite corner, turning left in the direction of the gas station. One step turned to two, which turned to ten as Patrick scanned the area for any sign of the people they were there to meet. A black woman talked on her cell phone as she pumped gas into a Civic. At the next pump, two teenaged boys talked beside a beat-up turquoise Camaro as they waited anxiously to continue their lives after such a menial task.

No teenaged boy with his father.

They stood off to the side, near the corner of the building and watched the traffic on the road beyond. A pickup truck, a beat-to-fuck Ford, a couple of motorcycles—the real kind, not the crotch rockets—but still no sign of anyone who fit Anthony's description of Jay.

Eight o'clock.
Eight ten.
Eight fifteen.
Still nothing.

Anthony fidgeted, putting his foot up behind him on the building, leaning, squatting on his heels, energy bursting from every inch of his five-foot-eight frame. The anxiety bled from him and into Patrick, and he hated it. He hated waiting for the world to end.

A car pulled into the gas station, headlights blazing in the low dusk. A monster of a car, it had once been something of an olive color, but dirt muted the shade. Patrick didn't know what kind it was, but it had to be something out of the seventies. Only SUVs were that big now. It pulled past the pumps and around to the parking spaces on the far side of the building. It didn't coast into one as Patrick expected, but cut across a couple, pointed at the exit. Patrick pulled out his phone and took a couple of sly pictures of the car and its plate. He wanted a few of the driver, but the passenger-side door was to him, and he couldn't get a clear shot.

Three people sat in the car, two in the front, one in the back. He could only see the passenger in the front seat clearly, a teenage boy with such emptiness in his eyes that it chilled him. The boy didn't look happy to see Anthony. He didn't jump out of the car with delight. Instead, he simply watched Anthony from the window.

The back door opened, and a voice called for Anthony to get in.

"Don't you fucking dare," Patrick grumbled at Anthony. "Don't you go anywhere near that car." He pushed Anthony back and approached the car, cell phone in hand. He got a glimpse of the dirty twentysomething guy in the backseat before someone yelled for Anthony again, an older, harder voice.

Patrick was standing two feet from the open door when the boy's eyes met his. He didn't speak, but a single tear ran down his cheek, glistening in the light of a nearby streetlamp. He was undoubtedly the kid from the picture in Anthony's backpack, everything from the curls to the eyes to the sorrow. He wanted to open the front door and pull the kid out, but the back door slammed in front of him and the car took off without another word.

ANTHONY

It hit the curb on its way out, bouncing into traffic with the whine of tires and the screech of a horn. After a minute, it was gone.

"I don't understand," Anthony said as he stepped up next to Patrick, whose heart thundered against his throat.

Patrick put an arm around Anthony's shoulders. They felt tiny under the weight of what could have happened to him had he been there alone. The guy in the back would have had no trouble pulling him into the car before they took off into the unknown.

"I don't know that I understand, either. Something isn't right."

"Thank you for being here."

"I'll always be here."

He walked Anthony back to the store, fending off Kevin, who always asked too many damn questions. Patrick watched Anthony go back up the aisle, stopping at one of the coolers for his pizza and a bottle of soda before heading upstairs.

At least he'd grabbed the food. That made the slump in Anthony's shoulders seem not so bad.

Patrick grabbed his cell phone as he climbed into the RAV4. He didn't bother texting but hit the speed dial to call his brother.

"Hey, what are you still doing at the store?"

"You remember that kid Anthony came here to see?"

"Yeah."

"He emailed Anthony and wanted to meet. I just went with him."

"I saw Anthony come back into the store. What happened? He looks... upset."

"If I didn't know any better, I'd swear it was a snatch and grab. It looked all kinds of skeezy, Bren. I don't know what the fuck is going on with that kid, but Anthony doesn't need to be anywhere near it."

"Snatch and grab, like they wanted to kidnap him?"

"It felt like that."

"Did you call the police?"

"And tell them what? It looked weird? They didn't actually do anything except try to pick up a kid who agreed to meet them."

"We should do something."

"Call that guy on the force that you're friends with. I'll send you the pics I took of the car."

"Okay." Bren's voice softened. "Is Anthony okay?"

"He's confused, like I am. But he took a pizza upstairs with him, so hopefully that means he's not too upset."

"I'll email him."

"I think that's a good idea."

Chapter Nineteen

Even in the light of day, Anthony had no idea what the fuck had happened the night before. Jay didn't even get out of the car to see him. No hugs, no excitement, not even a single word. If Patrick hadn't been there, he had no idea if he'd have gone with them. He hoped he wouldn't have. He hoped he had the sense enough to walk away, but the lost expression on Jay's face tore something in him. He wanted to grab Jay and let him stay in the apartment.

The computer dinged, and Anthony glanced down to see he had a new email. Nothing else had come in from Jay. Nothing at all had come in from anyone else in his family, including Allen. The only emails he got now were from Bren. He smiled at the subject line: *When the hell are you coming back?*

I don't have any friends. I don't have a lot of social skills.
I'm sorry I yelled at you about going out with that kid.
I thought it would mean you wouldn't come around anymore.
I like it when you come around.
Bring a fucking movie and come around.

Anthony hit the Reply button with a wicked grin.

Be a little more bossy next time.

The email dinged again.

Anthony Downing (which I had to learn from your email name, by the way), would you do me the honor of your company this evening for dinner? Beer, a pizza, and sex?

Cordially and horny,
Brendan Mears

Anthony snorted and tossed the cold pizza he'd been eating for breakfast back onto the cardboard circle.

Mr. Mears, I accept your gracious invitation. However, I'm really fucking sick of pizza. Can we do Chinese instead?

He waited a moment for the reply to come back.

Challenge accepted.

Since he had to work for most of the day, Anthony let Bren know he'd be there in the late afternoon. He threw the next *Harry Potter* movie into his backpack and tossed it into the corner for later. After a shower and grabbing the only clean outfit he had left, Anthony went downstairs for another day at the liquor store, wondering if he'd lose his virginity later that evening. In fact, he spent the rest of the day distracted by that very notion.

By five o'clock, Anthony and his dick were more than ready to spend an evening with Bren. He ran up the stairs two at a time to the apartment to retrieve his backpack. When he came back down, he was surprised to find Patrick waiting for him.

"Want a ride so you don't have to take the bus?" Patrick asked with a sly little grin.

"How did you know…? Bren told you I take the bus over to see him?"

"Yeah, he got on my ass about hooking you up with Sean. I asked how you guys had managed to get to know each other so well after a couple hours of waiting for the repair guy, and he told me about the movies. It's kind of you, Anthony."

Anthony's face heated at the mention of those couple hours spent waiting for the repair guy.

"Is that all he told you?"

"Hey, whatever *else* happens between you and my brother, I don't need to know." Patrick held his hands up in mock surrender, backing up to let Anthony pass on the way to the door. Anthony felt Kevin's eyes on him as they left. He climbed up next to Patrick in the RAV4 and they pulled out of the space.

"Does Kevin know Bren is gay?" Anthony asked as Patrick swung the truck out into the afternoon traffic.

"I don't know. I don't think it ever came up, why?"

"Nothing. You just kind of announced in front of him that I'm sleeping with your brother. Which I'm not, actually."

"Oh shit. I'm sorry. Let me know if he gives you any trouble, okay?"

"Okay. I was going to say that I can handle myself, but you're right. You should handle it since we're at work and you're his boss."

"Wait. Did you just agree to ask for help?"

"Yes, I did."

"Damn, there may be hope for you yet."

It only took a few minutes by car to get from the liquor store to Bren's house. They passed the time talking about a new promotion Patrick wanted to run and how Anthony thought they should set up the displays. He liked getting involved with setting up the displays, and Patrick thought he had a knack for it. When they pulled up in front of the house, Patrick mentioned maybe he should study advertising at Wayne State, the college Sean attended.

"It's a small school, probably more affordable than the gigantic state schools," Patrick told him. "You could look into severing your finances from your parents and see if you'd qualify for a grant."

Anthony pulled his backpack from between his feet.

"I don't know if I'd be able to afford school. I can't even afford to get my car fixed yet. But I'll talk to Sean and see what he thinks." He opened the door to get out.

"You know, Anthony, I went to college too," Patrick said with a frown.

"Yeah, but that was like *forever* ago."

"Hey!"

Anthony laughed as Patrick took a swipe at him from the driver's seat and he dodged behind the door. He had been considering college more and more since he'd gotten to Detroit. Being on his own had shown him, more than anything his parents or Aaron had ever said, that he'd need some kind of foundation if he wanted to start a life for himself. He threw the backpack over his shoulder and waved at Patrick before heading up the walk. The door opened before he knocked. A strong arm pulled him through and slammed it shut behind him.

His back hit the door and Bren's mouth covered his in an almost violent kiss before he'd even had time to breathe. Bren slid one hand behind his head to cradle it from hitting the wall while the other hand grabbed Anthony's ass, pulling their hips together. Anthony whimpered into the kiss, and Bren slid his lips to Anthony's cheek.

"Thank you for coming back," Bren whispered against his skin.

"Thanks for inviting me."

"You sure you'd rather be here with me than with pretty-boy Sean?"

"Ask me that again and I'm going to throat-punch you," Anthony growled and ran a finger over Bren's Adam's apple.

"It makes me hard when you threaten me like that."

"That's because you're a freak. Now feed me."

Bren laughed and gave him one final kiss before stepping back and pulling him by the front of the shirt into the kitchen. After forging in the kitchen for a few minutes, Bren came up with a menu from the Chinese place, and they sat at the table figuring out what they wanted to order. Anthony had never actually eaten Chinese food before. His parents didn't like it, and Chase never ate anything but fast food when they'd spent time at his house. So he went with Bren's recommendations, since Bren seemed to live on nothing but Chinese and pizza.

ANTHONY

Anthony popped in the movie and dropped the remote on the table while Bren ordered dinner. He felt more comfortable hanging out in this house than he ever had at home. Even though Bren didn't want to go outside, he loved the sunshine and left the curtains open, giving the room a light, airy feel. It seemed he'd been tense his entire life, but here, Anthony could relax.

Bren dropped down on the couch beside him, but instead of putting an arm around him or even just sitting together, he lay down and rested his head on Anthony's leg.

"You okay?" Anthony asked and ran a hand over Bren's shaggy hair.

"I didn't sleep well last night."

"Because of the argument?"

"That and your little rendezvous with your friend. Patrick told me how skeezy it was. I can't even think about something happening to you."

"I'm glad Patrick was there," Anthony admitted. "It made the whole thing not quite so scary."

"Let's not do either of those things again."

"Fight or get abducted?"

"Yeah, those."

"Deal."

Anthony continued to card his fingers through Bren's hair after he started the movie. Bren didn't have any questions as he normally did. In fact, he didn't say anything after the movie started. When Anthony leaned forward to see his face, he smiled at the calm serenity Bren had in sleep. It warmed something inside him that Bren trusted him enough to fall asleep in his lap. He watched Bren for a long while. Hell, he'd already seen *Goblet of Fire* a million times. Bren asleep on his leg brought him far more satisfaction.

He lamented the doorbell signaling the arrival of their food. Anthony couldn't get up with Bren in his lap, so he shook the man awake and went to pay the driver. When he returned, Bren had moved to a sitting position. Anthony grinned at the adorable way he stretched and yawned while Anthony laid out their food on the low table.

God, his mother would have a stroke if she knew he hadn't eaten in a kitchen for over a month.

"What's that grin for?" Bren asked as he piled a bit of sesame chicken on his plate.

"My mother was a stickler for eating in the kitchen or dining room. We were never allowed to have food in our rooms or the living room. Sitting here on the couch with you, I just realized I haven't eaten in a kitchen for over a month."

"You rebel."

"Right?" Anthony laughed again, and Bren beamed at him. At the same moment, they leaned toward each other, and their lips met in a slow, gentle kiss.

"Oh, I like that flavor," Anthony said as he licked at the sesame sauce Bren had left on his lips. "Put some of that on here." He lifted the plate, and Bren filled it with all the different things they'd ordered.

LATER, AFTER BELLIES were full and cartons had been stored in the refrigerator, Bren and Anthony sat watching the rest of the movie. Anthony had curled up in the corner of the couch with Bren's head in his lap. He'd considered making a joke about "while you're down there," but he liked just being with Bren, no sex needed.

When Anthony woke up hours later, only the DVD menu on the TV screen lit the room. Bren sat up and looked around, a little confused.

"What time is it?"

"I have no idea."

Bren reached in his pocket and grabbed his cell phone.

"Shit."

"What?"

"I have like ten missed texts from my brother and two missed calls. And it's after ten, so you've missed the last bus."

"Shit," Anthony agreed.

Bren slid his finger across the screen and tapped a few icons before holding the phone to his ear. He waited about thirty seconds before the call connected, then another thirty while Patrick said something loud and angry.

"Are you finished?" Bren asked and waited until Patrick stopped yelling. "Yes, he's here. We fell asleep on the couch watching a movie. No, neither of us are dead. No, you don't have to come out to the house in the middle of the night. He can stay here."

Anthony perked up at the pronouncement. Stay the night with Bren?

"He can either sleep in bed with me or on the couch, whichever he wants. And no, I'm not going to tell you which."

He couldn't help it, Anthony laughed at that. Bren looked at him with his eyebrows raised in question. Anthony nodded. Of course he'd stay.

"Yes, he said he'd stay. You can pick him up on the way in to the store tomorrow if you want." Again Bren looked to Anthony for confirmation, and again, he got it.

"Awesome. Good night, big brother. We'll name the first one after you."

Bren hung up before Anthony could hear a reply from Patrick, and they laughed.

"You don't mind staying here?"

"I'd love to. Wait, did that sound too eager? Did you want me to protest a little so I don't sound so easy?" Anthony batted his eyes, putting one coy finger under his chin. Bren busted out in a harsh laugh.

"I'm too tired to fuck you tonight, anyway. So there's no need to protect your virtue," he said with a smile, and then it fell, and he took one of Anthony's hands.

"What?"

"I don't know where this is going. I just... whether you want to just be fuck buddies, or friends, or whatever."

"I want the whatever," Anthony said without hesitation.

"I'm scared of the whatever," Bren admitted. "If we want something like that together, I think we should start out slow. I mean, yes, I want to take you to bed and fuck until neither of us can walk, but what then? I'd rather know you, and I'm starting to really get there." He ran a hand over his face. "God, did any of that make sense?"

"You want a real relationship with me. You're scared. You want to hold off on sex until we know each other better."

"Wow, you said that way better than I did."

"That's because I don't ramble."

"Shut up, take your pants off, and go get in my bed."

"I thought you just said...." Anthony laughed and dashed out of his reach before Bren could grab him. As Bren went to lock up the house, Anthony went into Bren's bedroom. Patrick had told him that it was Bren's childhood bedroom, that he'd always slept there. It housed a queen bed, dresser, and football posters that didn't really fit with the Bren he knew. The walls, a deep blue, contrasted sharply with the stark white ceiling. Every bit of wall space seemed to be covered with something—dresser, mirror, poster, and even a giant corkboard that held yellowing papers from a previous life. The bottles on the bedside table were recent, as were the clothes on top of the dresser. A mix of new and old that never quite meshed together into the person Bren had become.

ANTHONY

Anthony stood at the foot of the bed and unbuttoned his jeans. He didn't quite understand why he felt shy taking off his jeans when Bren had already sucked his dick. He dropped them to the floor and jumped into bed. A few moments later, the door opened and Bren stepped into the room. He watched Anthony for a long time, long enough it started to get uncomfortable. Then he watched him for another long moment.

"Is it wrong that I love the way you look in my bed?"

"Is it wrong that I love being in your bed?"

"You win that round."

Bren stood next to the bed and stretched as he pulled his faded Led Zeppelin T-shirt over his head. Anthony wanted to look away and give him privacy, the same privacy he'd had when he got undressed, but Bren held his gaze as he unbuttoned the worn jeans. He smiled as he pulled the zipper down.

"You know, for someone who doesn't want to have sex, you're being awfully flirtatious," Anthony said with fake annoyance.

Bren didn't answer. He just dropped his jeans with a wink, and the room heated ten degrees for Anthony. The man had long, toned legs that Anthony hadn't gotten to see when they'd been on the couch. Standing before him in just a pair of blue briefs, Bren was....

"Beautiful."

"Not really, just, you know, ignore the holes in my side."

Anthony tilted his head to look at Bren's side. He could see a small scar where the bullet had gone in and some scarring on the surrounding tissue.

"Can I see your phone for a second?" Anthony asked with a sudden idea.

"Sure." Bren reached to the side table and handed his smartphone to Anthony, who opened the browser and went to his Facebook page. He scrolled through the pictures. It took him a few minutes on the small screen, but eventually, he found what he'd been looking for and handed the phone back to Bren.

"That is my brother, Aaron. So trust me when I tell you, scars aren't a big deal for me."

Bren didn't say anything for a long time, just looking at the picture of the young man with the scars marring his handsome face. After a few minutes, he set the phone back down, climbed into bed under the covers, and opened his arms to let Anthony lie against his chest. He lifted just a bit as he twisted to turn off the side lamp. Then he wrapped both arms around Anthony, who could not get close enough.

I am home drifted through Anthony's mind as his last thought before he fell asleep.

Chapter Twenty

"Hey, could you turn on the television? I'll grab the movie from the bedroom." Bren pressed a small kiss to his temple, and Anthony smiled up at him.

"Sure you don't want me to go with you to get that movie?" He winked, and Bren laughed, not just a giggle or a snort, but an outright belly laugh. Anthony loved how his face lit up with that one simple act. As much as he understood why Bren wanted to wait and make sure they were starting on a solid foundation, God, he wanted to crawl in bed with the beautiful man and never come out again. He didn't want to think about school or his parents or the direction of his future except where it included Bren.

My boyfriend.

They hadn't talked about making anything official, but Anthony could feel it. Bren was the real thing.

Anthony grabbed the huge Sony remote from the low coffee table and hit the Power button. It took a minute for the screen to come on, and when it did, his heart stopped. A two-dimensional image of Jay staring back at him from the photograph he still had in his backpack made everything inside him freeze.

"Oh my God," Anthony said to no one and turned the volume up so he could hear the news report.

"The teenager, fifteen-year-old Rory Samuels, was found dead with a gunshot wound to the head, an apparent suicide, based on reports from neighbors who witnessed the incident."

"Okay, I—"

Out of the corner of his eye, Anthony saw Bren enter the room, but he couldn't turn. He couldn't take his eyes off that face on the screen. Anthony simply held up one finger, silently asking him to wait.

"In conjunction with the suicide, a Detroit native, fifty-two-year-old Jason Huehn, has been arrested and charged with two counts each of kidnapping and sexual assault. Huehn allegedly lured Samuels from his home in Columbus, Ohio, back in March, and held him against his will. Another teenager, a sixteen-year-old boy whose name is being withheld, was found locked in a basement room of Huehn's house."

The newscaster read the story in a detached voice, surrounding Anthony with cold. He didn't realize he was shaking until Bren wrapped strong arms around him.

"Shh... it's okay. It's okay, you're safe here," Bren whispered in his ear, and he almost believed it—until the next image appeared on the screen.

He barely recognized the skulking teenager filled with anger and rage. His mother must have taken it at some family gathering, because he recognized his backyard and a glimpse of his father in the background.

"Oh shit...." Bren's words were barely more than an exhalation.

"But tonight, we need your help. Another young man, eighteen-year-old Anthony Downing from DeKalb, Illinois, is also missing. Sources report Downing disappeared and may have been on his way to meet Huehn. If you have information on the missing teen, please call Crime Watchers at...." The sound faded as the blood roared in Anthony's ears.

"Oh Jesus," he whispered as his legs crumpled. Bren caught him and eased them both onto the sofa.

"Anthony...."

"He... he wasn't a kid. Jay wasn't.... He wanted to.... *Oh God.*"

"He didn't, Anthony. He didn't. You're right here with me. You're okay. It's going to be okay."

"The only reason he didn't rape me and keep me locked in his basement somewhere was because my car broke down. I... I could have been Aaron. I *would* have been Aaron."

The beautiful dinner Bren had made for him came bubbling up from his stomach, and he launched himself off the couch. He rounded the small table with the ugly vase and made it into the bathroom, where he dropped to his knees in front of the toilet as everything contracted and he vomited violently into the bowl. Bren came in right on his heels and lowered himself to the floor next to him, one hand rubbing lightly on his back.

He heaved again, and Bren's hand left his back. Acid burned his throat as wave after wave of stomach contractions pushed everything up and out into the toilet. A cold cloth touched the back of his neck, and finally, the violent rebellion of his body stopped. He didn't dare move, though, for fear it would start again.

Water ran in the sink as Bren wet the cloth again and then pulled on Anthony's shoulders, bringing his face away from the putrid smell of regurgitated pasta. Bren wiped Anthony's forehead, his cheeks, and then his mouth before throwing the rag up into the sink and pulling Anthony back against his chest. Bren lowered them so they rested against the tub, Anthony nestled in Bren's arms.

"We need to call the police station and let them know you're okay," Bren murmured against Anthony's hair as he stroked the side of Anthony's face. "There's a guy on the force we can call. He was good to me after the shooting. It will be okay. I'll be right here."

"I need to call them."

"The police?"

"My parents."

Anthony stayed in the safe, quiet circle of Bren's arms for a few long minutes before he crawled off the floor. His mouth tasted like stale shit, and it took an effort not to throw up again. Bracing himself with unsteady hands on the sink, he caught Bren's reflection in the mirror.

"Do you have any mouthwash, or something?"

Bren opened the medicine cabinet and brought out the open second half of a dual pack of toothbrushes and handed it to Anthony before picking up a tube of Crest.

"Do you want me to stay?"

Anthony nodded. He didn't know if he could be alone right then. None of the thoughts swirling in the tempest of his mind would slow long enough for him to catch them. He couldn't focus. Hell, he couldn't even breathe.

"Shhh...," Bren crooned in his ear, and as he leaned back into the safety of his boyfriend's arms again, Anthony hadn't even realized he'd dissolved into sobs. He spit the toothpaste out, rinsed with the cup of water handed to him, and tried not to choke.

They made it to the one room of the house where Anthony had most wanted to be for weeks, except Bren's blankets felt like sandpaper against his skin. The soft scent of Bren on the sheets helped to calm the live wires of his body as he nestled against the strong chest under his face.

He didn't know how long they lay together like that, but being held by Bren felt as right as anything Anthony had ever experienced. But they couldn't hide forever. The police were looking for him, and as soon as people started calling in to that number, they'd be looking for Patrick too.

"I don't want to call my parents."

"I know, but you have to let someone know you're okay. Anthony, I don't even know what I'd do if I couldn't find you, or Patrick went missing. After everything that's happened in our lives, it would destroy me. Even if your parents don't feel that way, I bet your brothers do."

"I just... I'm finally happy here. What if they make me go back to DeKalb?"

"Baby, they can't *make* you do anything. You're eighteen years old. You have a place to live. You have a job. You're fine right here. There is nothing they can do to make you leave."

Anthony took a deep breath and lifted his head to find Bren's worried gaze.

"You sure I'm worth the trouble?" Anthony whispered.

"I want you to have the world. I just hope there's room for me in it," Bren whispered back, and Anthony moved quickly, wrapping both arms around him, nuzzling into his neck.

"You're at the center of it."

They lay like that for a few more minutes, longer than Anthony intended to. He needed to call someone, and as much as he wanted it to be Allen, he knew Allen would try to talk him into coming home. Aaron was his only shot. Aaron would understand what it meant for him to finally be happy after all these years.

"Okay. I'm ready. Can I use your computer to get into my email? That's where all my phone numbers are stored."

Bren grabbed an iPad off his bedside table and handed it to Anthony. With quick efficiency, Anthony used the browser to access his email and then took the cell phone Bren held out for him. He typed in the number, hit Send, and held his breath.

It only took one ring.

"Hello?"

"Aaron?"

"Anthony? Oh God. Are you okay? Where are you?"

"I'm fine. I'm in Detroit."

"What? Why are you in Detroit? What happened? Mom said you ran away and then we're getting all these cops showing up about some rapist in Detroit. Are you safe? Where are you?" Aaron's words tumbled over each other, and Anthony took a long, slow breath.

"I was on my way to meet him. He made me believe he was a teenager. But my car broke down just outside Detroit, and I've been staying with a friend. I'm fine."

"A friend? What friend?"

"His name is Patrick."

"Okay, so, your car is broken down? I can send you money, or we can come and get you. You have a place to stay?"

"Yeah, Aaron. I've been staying in an apartment Patrick owns since I got here. I'm fine."

"An apartment Patrick owns? How old is this guy, Anthony? Are you okay?"

"He's thirty, and yes. I keep telling you that I'm fine."

"I'm at Mom and Dad's now. We're coming to get you. We'll pack a few things, and call Allen, and we'll be there. Just hold tight, Anthony, okay? Where are you?"

"Aaron, you're not listening to me. Fuck, no one *ever* listens to me. I'm *fine*, Aaron. I'm not coming home. I want to stay here. I'm happy here. I saw my face on the fucking news and wanted to tell you that I'm not dead."

"What do you mean you're not coming home? Of course you're coming home. You're a fucking kid, for Christ's sake." His voice muffled as he spoke away from the phone. "He's fine, Mom. Yes, I'll find out where he is."

"*You're not listening*," Anthony yelled. Bren put a hand on his leg.

"Do you have any idea what your little stunt did to Mom?" Aaron growled into the phone, his voice tight. "Do you even care? Where the fuck are you? Your friend's name and number just came up on my caller ID. You really think I can't use that to find you?" Aaron growled. "I can make a computer do fucking anything. Tell me where you are."

The tears came before Anthony could stop them. Bren reached for the phone, but he held up a hand. They were going to make him go back, no matter how miserable he was there.

"I'm staying in an apartment above Patrick's liquor store. Tonight I'll be staying with his brother, Brendan." Anthony looked to Bren, who nodded, then rattled off Bren's address and the address for the store. The place he knew by heart. The place that had become his home.

"That's fabulous. A recovering drug addict and alcoholic living above a liquor store."

"It's not like that. God, I fucking hate you. Do you know why I called you? Do you? I thought maybe out of all of them you'd understand that I'm happy now. I'm finally fucking happy. After being thrown down in that basement and forgotten about for years, finally, *finally* someone sees me. Someone cares what the fuck happens to me. You want to come, fine. Don't expect me to go home with you. I'm eighteen goddamn years old and can take care of myself."

Anthony screamed the last and hit the End button. He tossed the phone onto the bed before burying his face in his hands.

Chapter Twenty-One

Bren's heart ached as he held Anthony tight, trying to help contain the devastating sobs. They went on for what felt like hours, but in reality only lasted a few minutes. He stroked the shaggy brown hair that had started to become overgrown during Anthony's renegade summer in Detroit, leaving kisses between its strands. Anthony didn't want to go back to Illinois, and Bren didn't believe that was the best course of action, either. He wanted Anthony to stay, and not just because his heart ached at the thought of never seeing him again. They could get him enrolled in college, and he could build a life here. He could live, maybe for the first time in years, and if that life included Bren, even better.

"Okay, this is what we're going to do," Bren whispered against Anthony's hair. "It's only about six thirty, so we're going to call the police and let them know you're okay. They'll probably come and take a statement. You know that apartment is yours for as long as you want it. Patrick will say the same thing. You have a job. You have been talking about maybe going to Wayne State with Sean and the rest of your friends. You have friends here, Anthony, people who love you. We won't let them bully you into leaving. I'll take care of you. I promise."

"I don't want you to take care of me," Anthony said as he wiped his face on the bottom of his T-shirt and sat up. "We're supposed to be a team, not you taking care of the kid who can't handle shit."

"Hey, I never said you couldn't handle shit. I'm the one who can't handle shit. Today was a big fucking shock. Okay? I'm not sure how I would have handled it, either. All I'm saying is that you have options."

"And people who love me?" Anthony asked in a small voice.

"At least one person in this very bed."

"You love me?"

"Yep."

"Let's fucking get this over with. I want to take you to bed," Anthony said, and Bren laughed.

"Isn't that my line?"

"Dude, I don't care who says it as long as we end up in bed later. Naked. I'm going to go clean up a little so they don't think I'm actually homeless."

"I'll bring you a clean shirt."

"Thank you, Bren. You and Patrick saved my life. Not just from that guy, but in so many other ways. I love you." Anthony dropped a kiss on his cheek, and Bren laughed at Anthony's reluctance to kiss him after his bathroom escapades, even after he'd brushed his teeth.

"Thank you for picking our parking lot. You've changed my life too. Now I have something to live for."

"Stop, or we're going to end up in bed anyway, and we'll never put this shit behind us," Anthony said with a grin, the first since the news report started.

"If you want to take a shower, I can get you a towel."

"Nah, just the shirt. I'll take one later. We have at least five or six hours before my family descends on your house. God, I hope they at least wait until morning. It will be like one a.m. by the time they hit town."

"Text your brother and tell him your family can stay here if they want. I have two more bedrooms and a couch."

"They won't. They don't trust easily, not after what happened to Aaron."

"I'm okay with that too. Let them find a hotel."

Bren sat back against the headboard and patted the space between his legs for Anthony to sit. He wrapped his arms around the tiny scrap of a boy who had filled out into a handsome scrap of a man.

"You ready?"

"No, but let's do it anyway."

Bren pulled up Officer McClusky's number on his phone, a number he saw about once a month when Darren McClusky called to check in on him. Their dads had been friends, and Darren walked into the carnage of the store to get Bren out. He knew he could trust Darren with Anthony.

"Hey, Bren, what's up? You okay?"

"Yeah, Darren. I have a favor I need to ask you."

"Sure, man. What do you need?"

"So, the news just showed a missing kid. Anthony Downing, you heard anything about that?"

"Yeah, the whole station is buzzing about it. They just found out about him today when they started going through Heuhn's electronics. Do you know anything about him?"

"He's sitting right in front of me. His car broke down in the parking lot of the liquor store. Patrick kind of adopted him. He's been staying with us. We didn't know anyone was looking for him. I just wanted to let you know he's fine and he's at my house if you want to take a statement from him."

"He needs to come down to the station."

"That's the favor. I want to be with him. He had no idea Heuhn was a rapist. He's pretty shaken up about it."

"I get you." Papers shuffled on his end of the line. "Okay, let me talk to my captain. I don't think it will be a problem to do the interview there when I explain."

"Thanks, Darren."

He ended the call, and the two of them sat there, not speaking as the minutes ticked away. Bren didn't want to leave the safety of Anthony's warmth any more than Anthony did, who seemed happy to stay in the circle of Bren's arms. They were content to sit quietly among the smell of fabric softener from the freshly washed bedding, the gentle breeze coming in through the window, and most of all the rhythmic rise of fall of their own breathing.

"Can I ask you something?" Bren whispered against the shell of Anthony's ear.

"Always."

"How long have you had the money for your car?"

Anthony leaned to one side, turning his head so Bren could see his face. A small smile played across his lips even though his eyes were wide with surprise.

"How did you know?"

"I do the accounting for the store. Even if you'd been spending half of your paychecks, you'd have the money by now."

"I didn't want to tell Patrick I had the money because I was afraid...."

"Afraid he'd tell you it was time to move on?"

"Yeah."

"He'd never tell you that. You've become like another little brother to him. He wants you to stay almost as much as I do."

"Almost, huh?"

"No one wants you to stay as much as I do."

"I will. I just need to figure out what I'm going to do. When my mother sees that apartment with no appliances and barely electricity, she's going to freak."

"We'll figure it out."

ANTHONY

They stayed in bed, wrapped around each other, until a knock at the door broke them apart. Even then, Anthony looked at Bren one final time before they climbed off the mattress and headed for the living room. Bren looked back, and he could see his precarious sanity balanced on Anthony's trembling shoulders.

Bren watched for the next forty-five minutes as Anthony laid out the story for Darren and his partner Matt, a clean-cut black guy with hard eyes but a kind smile. They took him through it four or five times, each time getting a little more information from his tired, frightened memory. He sent them the messages from his Microsoft account. He told them about the botched attempt to visit "Jay" and how the plan was for them to meet in the deserted parking lot of the bookstore. Finally, he told them about the aborted pickup at the gas station, where Patrick's gut had saved Bren from having to see Anthony's picture in a completely different kind of news story.

"I just keep seeing that boy's haunted eyes. I should have seen it in the pictures he sent to me. I should have helped him," Anthony said, acknowledging the boy he thought had been Jay for the first time.

"You couldn't have known, Anthony," Matt said. He'd been quiet for most of the interview, interjecting a few clarifying questions between Darren's. "If you'd gone with them that day and tried to help...."

"Don't," Bren said to Matt, stopping whatever horrifying image he wanted to lay in their minds. Then, softer, he murmured to Anthony, "Patrick and I knew something wasn't right. We told Darren what happened that night, and they've been working on it. They just didn't get to him fast enough. That's not your fault. It's not our fault. It's not their fault. It's that man's fault. All of it."

They were quiet for a while. The mantel clock that had belonged to his mother was the only sound in the room, reminding them that time moves on, as life had shown Bren brutally, and so would they.

"Okay, I think we have what we need for now," Darren told Anthony gently. "How can we contact you if we need to get more information? I'm sure you're going to have to testify to all of this at the trial too."

"I'm staying in the apartment above the store. You can call me there, or here, I guess." Anthony recited both numbers from memory. It concerned Bren that Anthony still didn't have a cell phone. He'd have to add him to the store account once things calmed down. He couldn't stand to think about Anthony running around Detroit without any way to call for help. He hadn't had a way to call for help, and look where it got him.

"Okay. You said your parents are on the way?" Matt asked as he stood for them to leave, his pressed uniform pants starting to wrinkle around the edges so late in the evening.

"Yes," Anthony confirmed again. It was one of the first questions the officers had asked. "They should be here in a few more hours."

"Are you safe with them?" Darren asked, meeting Anthony's eyes.

"Yes. They didn't hurt me or anything."

"Not physically, anyway," Bren muttered, and Anthony slid a hand into his. He liked the way that felt. They didn't let go as Bren dragged Anthony with him to show the cops out. After the door closed behind them, he turned to Anthony.

"Have you heard from them yet?"

"I got a text from Aaron that they'd made reservations at some hotel in Royal Oak. That was as close as they could get. I told him I'd text him in the morning so we could make plans. I didn't know if you wanted them to come here, or if I should meet them at the store, or—"

Bren pulled his hand from Anthony's and cupped his face, sliding his thumb along the apple of Anthony's cheek. Nothing existed for him outside this moment. He knew that eventually, they'd have to deal with Anthony's parents and Patrick and more police, but then, right then, he wanted to hold on to the feeling of Anthony's skin.

"They can come here. I won't let you go through this alone."

"Thank you," Anthony whispered.

"Why don't we try to get some sleep? I know you said you wanted to get me into bed, but...."

"I'm exhausted, so yeah, I'd be happy to just sleep in your arms."

"I'd love that."

Chapter Twenty-Two

"Anthony, you're wearing a hole in the carpet," Patrick commented from the couch as Bren went into the kitchen to grab him another soda.

"You mean the hole right next to the beer stain hidden by an ancient floral rug?" Anthony popped another piece of toast into his mouth as he paced. His stomach wouldn't take anything more right then, but Bren had made him promise to eat something.

"He has a point," Bren said as he handed the fresh bottle to Anthony.

"He's just working himself up more by pacing. Are you sure you don't want some eggs or something?"

"No, I'll eat after. I promise. We can order up a pizza or something."

"You know it's eight o'clock in the morning? Besides, I've got frozen pizza in there. Just get through this, and we'll sit at the table laughing and joking and eating." Bren put his strong arms around Anthony's waist, and for the moment, everything calmed in the chaos of his mind.

Patrick brushed another imaginary piece of something off the front of his shirt, and Anthony cocked his head to the side.

"Why do you do that?"

"Do what?" Patrick asked, smoothing down his shirt.

"You brush the front of your shirt when you're nervous," Bren said, and Patrick looked confused.

"No, I don't."

"Yeah, right there on the side," Anthony said, pointing to the side of Patrick's shirt.

"Right where I was shot," Bren observed.

"What are you—?"

The doorbell rang.

Anthony didn't drop the soda only because Bren's arms were around him, but he startled so bad he moved them both.

"Anthony, you're an adult. You know you're safe here with us. There's nothing they can do to make you leave. Even if they take the car, you've been doing just fine without one." Patrick walked around where he and Bren stood wrapped around each other, headed for the door. "Are you guys ready?"

"Let's get this over with." Anthony stepped out of the comfort of Bren's arms and stood next to him quietly as Patrick opened the door. His mother came through first, searching the small living room and then, in two bounding steps, pulled him into her arms.

"Oh my God, I thought something had happened to you. I… couldn't. Why, Anthony? Why would you do this? Leave without a word? We were worried sick. Allen is on his way up. He should be here in an hour or so. Thank God Aaron was already there. We could leave in a hurry. Your father just threw things in the car and we left." She rambled on as she checked him over for signs of injury.

"Mom," he said quietly. "I'm fine."

"No, you're not fine. You've been out here all on your own and that man…. Did you ever have contact with him, meet him? God, when I think about what could have happened to you." The tears started then. He appreciated her holding them at bay for that long. She dissolved on his shoulder, and he noticed she seemed a few inches shorter. That's when he realized he'd grown in the weeks since he'd seen her. Anthony looked over his mother's shoulder and caught Aaron's gaze. The neutrality of it gave him strength.

"Mom, I am fine. He didn't do anything to me, and I have friends here who have helped me since I got here. This is Bren." Anthony reached out, took Bren's hand, and held it tightly. Then he nodded at Patrick. "And this is his brother Patrick. My car broke down in their parking lot, and they helped me. Then we became friends."

Anthony's mother stared at Anthony and Bren's joined hands, and he felt the heat rise in his face.

"And Bren and I have become more than friends."

"I don't... I don't understand. You're gay? Anthony?"

"Yes. Just like Aaron. I've known for years."

"Why didn't you say anything? How did I not see this?" She asked the questions apparently to no one, since she looked only at her wringing hands.

"Because, after Aaron got hurt, you never saw me. Allen knew I was gay. I don't know if Aaron did or not. He was pretty caught up in his own head."

"Mrs. Downing, would you and your family like to sit down so we can talk?" Patrick asked and waved his hand around the living room, indicating the couches and the extra chairs he and Bren had brought in from the garage.

Stunned into silence, his mother moved over to one of the couches, flanked by Aaron and their father. Bren and Anthony took the love seat, and Patrick took the wingback chair. The other chairs sat unused like an absent audience. Bren didn't let go of Anthony's hand but rested their clasped hands on his leg.

"How about you take us through it, sport?" his father asked, speaking for the first time.

"You call me that like I'm still twelve, Dad." Anthony took a deep breath and wondered where to begin. Should he tell them about the party? About Chase? Everything in his life had led up to this moment. He decided to start at the point where his story really began.

"When I was ten years old, the world changed. My big brother turned into a different person, and I got thrown into the basement where the monsters were. I was scared of every noise, every shadow. It took years before I was able to really sleep again. By then I'd started drinking so I could make it through the night." Anthony didn't look at his father, or his mother. His gaze remained fixed on Aaron. Aaron would understand, at least this part. "Then, Allen left and Aaron left and I was all alone. I felt more alone than I thought possible."

"Why didn't you come and talk to us about it?" His father reached out a hand to him but then pulled it back when he realized Anthony wasn't interested.

"Because, by then, I was just another broken kid right out of rehab. The only time you ever talked to me was to tell me to get my shit together and go to college. It felt like you couldn't wait to get rid of me."

"Anthony—"

"Please let me finish." He drew in a shaky breath. "The night before I left for Detroit, I snuck out and went to a party with Chase. Only by then, it wasn't really sneaking out because no one cared if I was there or not. Anyway, we went to this party and something happened between us. Something sexual. I'll spare you the details."

Bren shifted on the couch, and Anthony tightened his grip on Bren's hand.

"He… he told everyone at the party what happened and was cruel about it. When I got home, I was upset and angry. I couldn't sleep. I logged on to my Xbox, and Jay messaged me like he always did. He told me that he wouldn't hurt me, that he cared about me. I was so sick of being invisible and unwanted. When he said I should come to Detroit and stay with him for the summer, I didn't think about the consequences. I just packed up the car, and I went."

Anthony left out the part about stealing from them so he didn't have to tell Bren and Patrick. That moment felt like a lifetime ago. He wasn't that angry kid anymore.

"Anyway. There was some construction on the highway and I got diverted. The car was acting up, and I got off to get gas. When I started out of the gas station, my transmission blew and I coasted into the parking lot at the liquor store."

Anthony could still feel the terror of that moment, not knowing what he should do or where he should go.

"I didn't know what to do. It was late, and I hadn't slept the night before. I rolled the windows up and locked the doors, and then I tried to sleep. Patrick woke me up the next morning, banging on the window to see if I needed help. He called a mechanic friend of his to look at the car and then offered me a place to stay and a job while I saved up the money to fix the transmission."

"I don't understand, Anthony. Why didn't you call us if you were in trouble?" His mother's tone of voice begged him for answer, her voice breaking with the strain of the accusation in those words.

First Anthony looked at Patrick, whose earnest and kind eyes met his.

Then he looked at Bren, who smiled in that soft, secretive way.

Finally, he opened his mouth and said the words that would make them all hate him.

"I stole money from your room in order to make the trip. I figured you didn't want to have anything to do with me after that. Your kid was an alcoholic, a drug addict, and a thief. Aaron pretty much nailed it on the phone last night."

He looked away from Bren, away from Patrick, away from all of them and stared at a picture of a much younger, smiling Bren and Patrick sitting on the shelf across from him.

"Anthony, had I known you were leaving, I'd have given you the damn money. You really think a couple hundred dollars was worth more to me than the safety of my son? Is that how little you think of me?" his mother asked, clutching at his father's knee.

The burning that had been welling in Anthony's throat won out, and tears slipped down his face.

"I don't want to do this anymore. I don't want to feel like this. God, all I wanted was peace." He turned and buried his face against Bren's chest.

Patrick stood up. "Okay, why don't we take a break for a few minutes? Would any of you like something to drink? We have soda, tea, water, and Bren probably has some coffee in there." He waited next to the chair for someone to break the terrible tension choking them all.

"I'll take a soda, Sprite or Coke if you have it," Aaron finally said, and Anthony looked up at his brother.

"Sure, I'll take some coffee if you find some," his father offered. "And I think Michelle could do with a little too, if it's not too much trouble."

Patrick escaped the room, and Anthony imagined him filled with more glee than he had a right to. Bren simply stayed still, continuing to hold Anthony against his warm, safe chest.

"You're not going to hate me because I stole money to get here?" he whispered to Bren. "Maybe you won't be able to trust me again."

"Hey, none of that. You were a scared kid looking for a way out. You're so much different now than when you rolled into that parking lot. I hope you see it." Bren kissed his forehead, and Anthony took a full breath again.

"What about you?" he asked Aaron.

"If that's the worst thing you do in your life, I'll be a happy person." He shrugged. "I'm more pissed off at you for what you put our family through in the last few months."

"I can accept that," Anthony admitted. "If you accept that I'm pissed off at you for what you put me through for the past eight years."

"I've always accepted that. You've hated me since you were fourteen. I accepted it a long time ago."

"I don't hate you. Okay, maybe I did. But I don't anymore. I'm happy you found Spencer and a way to have a life again. Speaking of, where is Spencer? Is he okay?"

"Yeah, I was just staying with Mom and Dad because he's in California. His aunt Nell had a baby girl. He went out to help and see them."

Anthony almost smiled at that. "That's sweet. It sounds like you guys are really settling in. Happy." His smile fell away. "I'm just hoping you'll see that I'm happy too."

"Okay, then, when your friend comes back in here, tell us about it." Aaron leaned back to rest against the back of the couch. Anthony could tell his brother had taken something to deal with the changes he'd had to endure in the past few hours. He tried to hold on to his anger, but gratitude took its place.

They didn't talk while Patrick made coffee and shuffled sodas to Aaron and Bren. Anthony grabbed his too, just for something to hold in his hands while they waited. Finally, after time had solidified and beat them to death with the creamer spoon, Patrick came back in with a tray holding three cups of coffee and various accessories. He'd just set it on the low table in front of the couch when the doorbell rang again.

"It's Allen," Aaron confirmed.

Anthony got up to open the door while Patrick served his parents coffee they probably wouldn't drink. He didn't want to face Allen's wrath, not after Aaron, not after his mother. He stretched out the walk to the door as long as he could, but eventually, he reached it. The knob had barely turned in his hand before his brother stood before him on the porch. He didn't get a word out before Allen threw his arms around Anthony and held on for all he was worth.

"You scared the hell out of me," Allen whispered, and even with the barely-there sound, he could hear Allen's tears. "I thought something had happened to you. It almost killed me." He let Anthony go and stepped back just enough to see his face. "I thought we were a team? Why didn't you call me? Why?"

Anthony couldn't stop the racking sobs as he grabbed his brother again. There were no words, just terrible painful waves of anguish and regret. The one person in his life who had been there for him, and Anthony had let him down. He didn't regret his choice, though. That choice had led him to Bren and to Patrick and Sean and Sandy and all the other friends he'd made there. He had more friends in their quiet little Detroit suburb than he'd ever had back home.

"I needed a life of my own. It didn't work out the way that I planned, but this is a good place for me. I fit here. I've never fit anywhere," Anthony whispered. "Please don't be mad. I'm sorry I scared you. I just... I needed to get out. You know what that feels like."

"Yeah, I do." Allen pulled back to wipe his eyes on his shirt. "So, can we come in?"

"Sorry," Anthony laughed, for what seemed like the first time in days. He stood back to let Allen come in with a woman Anthony didn't quite expect. They met eye to eye, being the same height, but the similarities ended there. The pale silk scarf she wore against a soft, pink sweater gave her an air of sophistication. Long legs filled out perfectly fitting jeans leading to warm leather boots absent of scuff or wear.

"Anthony, this is Melanie. Melanie, this is my younger brother Anthony." The adoration in Allen's voice was surpassed only by the emotion of his gaze as he looked at her.

"It's a pleasure to meet you," she said with a soft smile, holding out a well-manicured hand. Anthony took it, not sure if he should shake it or kiss it.

He went with the former.

Allen slid his hand to Melanie's lower back, and they stepped past him and into the living room as Anthony closed the door and turned back to the insanity that had befallen Bren's home. If he hadn't convinced Anthony of his love last night, Anthony might have wondered if they'd make it past this. But in his heart, he didn't even worry.

"Mom, Dad, Aaron, this is Melanie," Allen introduced again, and their mother stood to give Melanie a hug while his father and Aaron hung back. His dad shook her hand, but Aaron just gave her a half wave. She smiled gently at him, the same smile Darren had given Bren last night. It looked like an "I have no idea what to say to you, so I'm just going to smile awkwardly" kind of thing, and he wondered just how often people treated Aaron like that. It hurt his soul to think of people constantly giving Bren that smile.

While his parents talked with Melanie, cutting through the tension, Bren wrapped his arms around Anthony from behind and kissed him just below the ear. Patrick smiled at them from behind his coffee cup. In that moment, Anthony knew he would be okay.

Anthony's mother talked with Melanie about nothing while Aaron quietly relayed to Allen what had happened to that point. He heard the word *boyfriend* as they looked up at Bren. It shocked him to hear the words *seems to be doing better* as he led Bren back to the love seat. They sat down, and Bren put an arm around him, surrounding him with warmth, encouragement, and the delicate scent of woodsy spice Anthony loved.

Their return to the circle seemed to be the cue for things to continue. Allen and Melanie pulled up a couple of the vacant folding chairs and sat next to Patrick for their little Anthony-intervention. Allen reached over to hold Melanie's hand, bringing his abstract girlfriend into their concrete world. At almost the same time, he also noticed that his parents weren't touching. He didn't know what that meant.

"So, what happens now?" Allen asked, brutally cutting through to the heart of the matter. They'd told their stories. They'd shed their tears. Now it was time to take action.

Their mother started to say something, but Aaron put a hand on her arm.

"What are *your* plans, Anthony?" The room held a collective breath as Aaron tossed the question out like a grenade, waiting for the shrapnel to pierce them all.

"I'm staying here. Patrick said I can keep working at the liquor store and take on more responsibility when I turn twenty-one. We're going to work on the apartment above the store and make it more of a permanent place to live. I'm also going to apply to Wayne State. I have friends there, and they say it's pretty gay-friendly. I don't know what I'm going to major in yet, but the first year is all foundational crap anyway so I have a bit of time to decide." Anthony rattled everything off in a hurry, feeling distinctly nervous at the reddening hue of his mother's face. She looked like an old *Tom and Jerry* cartoon he used to watch as a kid, as Tom's head turned into a teakettle before he exploded in a shrill whistle.

"I am not going to let my eighteen-year-old son live above a liquor store in Detroit. It's ludicrous. If you want to go to college, that's great. We want you to go to college. We'll find a college that works for you once you figure out what you want to do."

"There are actually two sets of locks between him and the outside in that apartment," Patrick put in, his voice even. "There's the one on the front door with a motion-sensor alarm and then there's another on the apartment itself. So, actually, he's safer there than he would be in a dorm or other apartment."

"He wouldn't be safer than he is at home," she countered.

"Actually, none of us are safe anywhere," Aaron said quietly. "I lived in that house all my life and I wasn't safe."

"No, you are not ganging up on me, not about this," his mother said, managing to wag a finger at them.

They started to squabble among themselves, and Anthony sighed. He had no intention of letting them talk him back to DeKalb. They had no way to force him. The clock ticked away on the bookshelf as they argued, and he'd almost decided to say something when Bren cleared his throat.

"Look, I know just like Aaron does that no one is safe anywhere. Is your only objection to him staying here with us that you don't want him living above the store?" Bren asked in a low, steady voice.

"It's not the only reason, but it's a big one," his mother admitted.

"Okay." Bren turned slightly so his upper body faced Anthony. He smiled, and the world seemed to brighten with that one simple act. With his free hand, Bren took Anthony's and entwined their fingers. Anthony looked at them and then back up into Bren's face.

"What would you think of moving in with me? Roommates, boyfriends, whatever—I like having you here." Bren stroked the back of Anthony's hand with his thumb.

"How's he going to get to work?" Patrick chimed in, not in a harsh way, but more trying to work the problem.

"Anthony's had the money to fix the car for weeks."

Patrick stared at Anthony, and then his family turned to stare at Anthony. The room heated inexorably as Anthony blushed.

"You have?"

"I didn't want to leave." The words came out as no more than a whisper, but everyone in the room seemed to hear them. They sat back in their chairs, still looking at Anthony. He felt as though he'd accidentally stood in front of the television during the final out of the World Series.

"So, you would have just... what? Kept Sandy waiting forever?" The humor in Patrick's voice took the sting out of the words.

"I was just giving myself a little time. I had a pretty good idea that you'd let me stay and you weren't looking for a new stocker, so I hoped you'd let me keep my job. Sean and I went to Wayne State and got a package for enrollment. I was just trying to figure out what to do about the FAFSA forms without my parents' information." Anthony shrugged and glanced at his parents.

"You didn't answer my question." Bren nudged Anthony's arm and planted a kiss on the side of his hair.

"You really want me to move in with you?" He couldn't keep the hope out of his voice.

"I have a ton of space, and it will be nice not to be alone in this house anymore."

Bren touched his face, and Anthony nodded as his mother sat forward.

"Anthony, I don't think that's a—"

"Melanie's pregnant. We're getting married," Allen announced, and the room fell silent for exactly thirty seconds before chaos ensued.

"You're too young to start a family. You haven't even graduated from college," his mother cried, grabbing their father's hand for the first time, as though she just couldn't take anymore.

"No, I haven't, but I have a good job and I can do college for a year and work. It's one year. Then I'll have a foundation to take care of my family." Allen turned his head to Melanie, who smiled at him. The adoration between them made Anthony's breath catch. He hoped one day, he and Bren might have that same deep connection, something more than love, something foundational.

"When.... When were you planning to get married? We have to have time to plan."

"Oh, we were just going to go to the justice of the peace and—"

"You will not," his mother said. "Even if we have it in the backyard, you are going to have a proper wedding. You guys are working together to give me a coronary. It's just like when you were boys." She leaned against their father and wondered aloud if Patrick had any Bailey's she could add to that coffee before they dropped any more surprises on her.

Patrick stood up and went into the kitchen.

"Well, Mom, look on the bright side. At least Aaron can't knock up Spencer," Allen said with a laugh. Anthony snorted. Allen had always come to the rescue with him, and with Aaron.

Then the reality of what Allen said hit him.

"I'm going to be an uncle?" Everything in the room brightened with that single thought.

"That you are, little brother."

"Hey, Aaron, didn't you say Spencer's aunt had a baby? When you get married, won't that make you a...."

Aaron rolled his eyes.

"I'm not talking about marriage anytime soon, and that would make her Spencer's cousin."

"Awwww. I can just see you playing with a baby."

"No, you can't."

"What's her name?"

Despite his grumbling, Aaron smiled then. "Her name is Sophie."

Chapter Twenty-Three

It took a while for Anthony's family to leave his house, and Bren appreciated the silence. At one time, the house had been filled with chatter and laughter, but slowly, it had turned into a mausoleum. Maybe Anthony would be able to help him change that.

Maybe he already had.

Anthony had started to clean up the plates and cups in the kitchen. Something inside Bren swelled as he watched. Well, something in his pants swelled too, but that was a completely different thing.

Bren liked having Anthony there, though he noticed that during the conversation with his parents, Anthony had never actually agreed to move in with him. Because of the chaos of the talk, and the stress of his parents, Bren had let it go, but it niggled at him, like things often did when he dwelled on them longer than he should. So he hoisted himself off the couch and joined Anthony in the kitchen.

"You only put your arms around me to keep from doing dishes," Anthony admonished with a laugh as Bren wrapped his arms around Anthony's waist. He kissed the back of Anthony's neck, eliciting a shiver that made him hard.

"Yep."

"There isn't much here; I'll have them in the dishwasher in a minute. You want to watch a movie?" Anthony asked as he rinsed another plate and stacked it to go into the machine. He smelled like Bren's soap, and Bren kissed him again.

"I want to start watching a movie. Then I want to give up on it because we were making out too much to pay attention. After that, I want to spend the rest of the afternoon in bed making you moan my name."

"Then get out of my way so I can load the damn dishwasher and we can get started."

Bren laughed and released Anthony from his grip. He liked this Anthony, the fun-loving, free-spirited guy he had become. The lonely, angry teenager had slipped into his past like the football-playing, business major had slid into Bren's. They were different people, maybe even the people fate intended them to be. And at least for a while, they were happy.

"There's something else I wanted to talk to you about," Bren said, pulling up his big-boy pants. He'd been researching and talking about it with Patrick, but he hadn't brought it up to Anthony because he didn't want to get his boyfriend's hopes up. He didn't know if it would work. He didn't know if they'd be able to be a normal couple one day.

Anthony stalled, and Bren wondered what he thought the talk could be about. Finally, he put the last of the dishes into the machine and turned around. His eyes stayed locked on the front of Bren's shirt.

"Whatever you think this is about, you're probably wrong," Bren said, putting a finger under Anthony's chin and lifting it until their eyes met.

"Okay. Then what is it about?"

"Wait, what do you think it's about first?" Bren asked with real curiosity.

"That maybe you were hasty in asking me to move in with you and you'd changed your mind."

"Hold on, is that why you haven't answered me yet? You think I'm going to change my mind?"

Anthony didn't say anything, but the worry in his face screamed his agreement more than any vocal admission.

"Anthony, I really want you to move in with me. It wasn't just a knee-jerk reaction to your parents freaking out. I just didn't know how to ask you because I figured you had better options than being locked up with the freak who can't leave." Now it was Bren's turn to look away.

"Yes, I'll move in with you," Anthony said and took Bren's face between his hands. The resulting kiss brimmed with hope and love and promise.

"Wow," Bren whispered when it finally ended.

"Now, what did you want to talk to me about?"

Bren took a breath and then laced his fingers with Anthony's as they faced each other between the sink and the table.

"I've been looking online and talking to Patrick. I think I want to try working with a therapist. You deserve more than someone who is trapped in the house by their own head. I want to be that guy."

Anthony touched Bren's cheek. "First, you can't take on therapy because of me. It won't work. If I learned anything from years of living with Aaron, therapy has to be something you want. Second, I like you just the way you are, Bren. If I didn't, I wouldn't be here. You are the guy I want to be with now; you don't need to change. Finally, I will stand by your side, whatever decision you choose. I see what the right therapist has done to help Aaron, and it's been like night and day. I want that for you, not because I want you to change, but because I want you to look in the mirror and like the guy you see. I want you to be able to go out and enjoy the sunshine or catch a Lions game if you want. Not for me, but for you."

"Fuck the movie," Bren breathed and wrapped his strong arms around Anthony. He lifted Anthony so he had no alternative but to wrap his legs around Bren's waist. Their kiss started in the kitchen, but after slamming his knee into the doorframe and Anthony's head into a low-hanging lamp in the hall, he sat Anthony back on his feet and just held his hand until they reached the bedroom. He stopped and turned.

"Are you sure you want to do this? We don't have to. We can just mess around like we always do."

"I want to do it, and I want it to be with you. Now stop stalling and strip."

Bren laughed and pulled him inside the room to shut and lock the door. He didn't know why. Even when he was alone in the house, he locked the bathroom door. Maybe it was because he could never know who might walk in through the door or the carnage they could bring. Since the shooting, Bren liked locked doors.

He took off his shirt first. In the harsh light of afternoon, he hated the way his body looked since his life had atrophied. During high school, he'd worked hard to build his body up. But after two years of apathy, he felt small and weak. It didn't matter before; no one saw it. But now Anthony did see it, and Bren hated it. But then he noticed Anthony's hungry expression, and his self-doubt faded to a quiet hum instead of a roar.

Anthony stripped out of the nice button-down Patrick had lent him for the standoff with his parents. With each successive button, Bren's mouth went just a little drier. The undershirt came next, and Bren's hands froze on the button of his jeans while he watched. In the oversized clothes he wore, Anthony seemed small and waifish. Now he was out of them, Bren wanted nothing more than to trace the lines and contours of that sweet body with his mouth.

Bren stepped forward and pulled Anthony to him by the waistband of his jeans. He didn't want to wait anymore. Their kiss melted all the tiny little places inside him that were still frozen by fear and doubt. Their mouths opened and closed against each other again and again, and Bren felt Anthony moan into his mouth. It made the ache in his cock ten times worse... or better. Anthony's hands were on his ass before he could blink, and he reached between them to get their pants out of the way before his brain exploded.

When they kicked out of their jeans and underwear, Bren stopped Anthony from climbing onto the bed.

"What?" Anthony asked. "Don't you want...?"

"I do. It's awkward-conversation time."

"Another one?"

"Tell me what you want to happen."

"I want to have sex."

"How?"

"What do you mean, how? Insert tab A into slot B.... Repeatedly."

"Who is the tab and who is the slot?"

"Did you just call me a slot?"

Bren broke then and sat on the edge of the bed laughing. Anthony put a hand on his shoulder. He tried not to notice Anthony's naked dick bobbing in front of his face.

"I cleaned up earlier because I want you to fuck me," Anthony said. "Does that make it easier?"

Instead of responding, Bren inched forward on the bed and pulled Anthony's cock into his mouth. Anthony's hands rested on his shoulders, and he loved the contact between them. Nothing heavy, just gentle touches of affection. Anthony didn't try to grab Bren's head or thrust his hips but took what Bren gave him. It only lasted a few minutes, though, until Bren couldn't stand it anymore and needed Anthony to be under him.

"Should I lie on my back, or...?" Anthony's shyness seemed to return with the close proximity of having sex for the first time. Bren pulled Anthony down next to him onto the bed. They lay on their sides, facing each other, with no space between them—chest to chest, hip to hip, legs entwined. Bren had never really lain with someone so close it felt as if they were a single person, and he kissed Anthony slowly in thanks.

They kissed for a while longer, until the tension in Anthony's body stretched into coarse sexual need. He rubbed his hips against Bren, almost begging for him to take them further. Anthony went eagerly when he rolled them and planted his hands on either side of his boyfriend's head. He rolled his hips against Anthony.

"Are you sure?"

"Will you get the lube already?"

"Impatient little thing, aren't you?" Bren leaned over to his nightstand and found the lube he'd been using to jack off. Anthony ran his bare feet over the sides of Bren's hips, spreading himself open as Bren rubbed his dick just behind Anthony's balls.

"I haven't been with anyone since the shooting," Bren whispered.

"I trust you. I don't want to use a condom unless you do," Anthony whispered back, as if speaking would ruin the moment with more awkward decisions. Bren nodded and sat up on his knees between Anthony's open thighs. He couldn't articulate how hot Anthony looked, though he wanted to. Dribbling a bit of lube on his fingers, he slid them over Anthony's hole before it had the chance to drip on the bed. Not that Bren cared about the sheets. He just wanted his fingers inside Anthony.

The quiet whimper that escaped Anthony's lips as Bren's fingers penetrated his ass made Bren want to drive his cock so deep into him that they'd never separate again. He held on to that need, tucking it inside himself as he gently rubbed lube around the rim of Anthony's entrance, hot and tight against his fingers. His boyfriend writhed against his hand, arching his back to take the fingers deeper.

"Do you like that?" Bren asked, as almost at the same time Anthony started to stroke his softening cock.

"There's some pain, but I like the stretch and knowing you're touching me like that."

"Fucking your ass with my fingers?"

Anthony moaned and pulled his dick a little faster. Bren grabbed the lube with his free hand and poured a little over the peek-a-boo head of Anthony's cock as it popped in and out of his fist. He'd need that later anyway, once Bren buried himself balls deep and they were both desperate to come.

"Try another." Anthony opened his eyes and looked up at Bren. "Then I think we can try. The burn feels good when I'm jacking off."

"Okay." Bren did as Anthony asked and slid his ring finger in next to the other two. Anthony's eyes slammed shut, and he moaned again, a guttural thing that made Bren's skin tingle. He watched Anthony's hand race over his cock, twisting over the head while his hips writhed. Fuck, if he came, Bren would too.

Anthony's eyes opened as if waking from a dream, and he pushed Bren's arm back, dislodging his fingers. Then he pulled Bren down on top of him.

"Please, Bren, please fuck me," he whispered against the shell of Bren's ear, and the pleading note made everything in him tighten. Bren reached between them and grabbed his own dick. He rubbed it against Anthony's body and searched with his fingers until he found that tight little hole. With an ache that radiated through his core, Bren slid the head into Anthony's body with reverence. The need of it made the backs of his teeth grind, but he forced himself to go slow. Anthony's breathless whimper didn't help anything.

"Give me a second," Anthony moaned and moved his hips a fraction, then a bit more. Bren balled his hands into fists, dropping to his forearms beneath Anthony's shoulders. He pressed his forehead into the side of Anthony's neck and waited. The body beneath his moved again, harder, plunging his cock deeper, and his toes curled.

"Please," he whispered against Anthony's skin.

"Okay," Anthony conceded, and Bren pushed forward with torturous slowness. When Anthony didn't protest, he pulled out and did it again. Then faster. With Anthony's mouth near his ear, Bren heard every sound that came out of him. Every fucking sound. They drove him insane with the need to slam into Anthony.

After a minute of awkward maneuvering, they came together in a slow rhythm. Push and pull, yin and yang, in and out, the same steps of a centuries old rhythm. Then Anthony kissed the side of his face.

"I love you," he whispered, and any control Bren ever possessed broke in that instant. He wrapped his arms tightly around Anthony to hold on for the ride and threw himself into their lovemaking with abandon. He drove into Anthony, who cried out, not in pain, but in need. The sheer want in his voice made Bren crazy.

"Anthony," Bren whispered over and over as the friction and heat sent him spiraling, racing toward climax. Anthony clenched the back of Bren's hair with his free hand, and Bren pulled back, but Anthony's legs wrapped tight around his waist, tugging him closer instead. He covered Anthony's mouth, lost in the kissing and the heat of his lover's body. When he could no longer contain it, he jerked his arms from under Anthony's shoulders and put them on either side of his head, cradling him, as Anthony wrapped his arms around Bren.

They were one.

Anthony came first, the heat of it splashing on Bren's abs as well as his own. He loved the cry Anthony made, soundless at first and then a whine of release. As Anthony fell back against the sheets, Bren didn't slow; he raced toward his own finishing line, tightening everything in a desperate suspension of time.

"Bren," Anthony whispered. Bren's body took over, driving relentlessly, harder, deeper, until everything exploded in shards of color and he came inside Anthony's hot, tight body. He tried to fall to the side, but Anthony pulled him down like a blanket.

"That was.... God, that was amazing," Anthony said against his cheek between slow, distracted kisses.

"It's always been fun and got me off, but it's never been that intense for me," Bren admitted. "I've never been in love with the guy I'd fucked before."

"Can we just stay here for, maybe, two or three weeks? Just like this?" Anthony asked with a laugh.

Bren cupped Anthony's face in his hands and placed a gentle kiss upon his lips.

"We can stay like this forever."

THE END

Don't miss out!

Visit the website below and you can sign up to receive emails whenever JP Barnaby publishes a new book. There's no charge and no obligation.

https://books2read.com/r/B-A-EBYTC-ZAWHF

BOOKS 2 READ

Connecting independent readers to independent writers.

Did you love *Anthony*? Then you should read *Spencer*[1] by JP Barnaby!

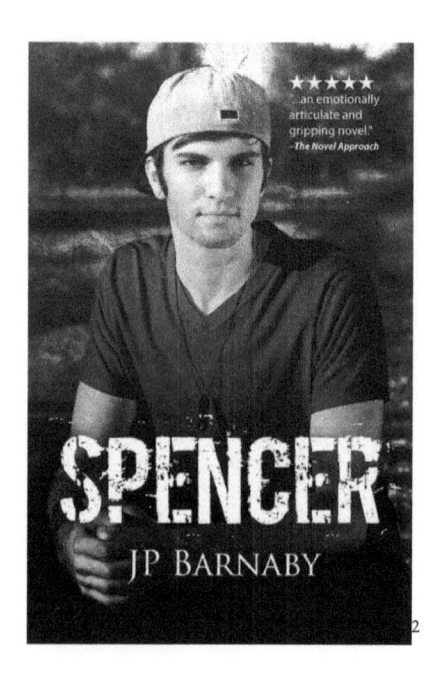

It's been nearly five years since Aaron woke up in the hospital so broken, he couldn't stand the sight of his own face. The flashbacks no longer dominate his life, but he's still unable to find intimacy with his lover, Spencer Thomas. With time, patience, and the support of his family, his therapist, and his loving partner, Aaron has figured out how to live again. The problem is, Spencer hasn't. His life has been on hold as he waits for the day he and Aaron can have a normal relationship. Hoping to move things forward for them both, he takes a job as a programmer in downtown Chicago, leaving Aaron alone.

Reeling in the wake of Spencer's absence, Aaron receives another shock when his attackers are caught.

---

1. https://books2read.com/u/4Ev8o0
2. https://books2read.com/u/4Ev8o0

Now, he must testify and verbalize his worst nightmare. Publicly reliving his trauma without Spencer at his side destroys his precarious control. But he finds someone who can understand and empathize in Jordan, who watched his brother cut down in a school shooting. With Spencer gone and the DA knocking at his door, Aaron seeks solace in Jordan, and Spencer will have to risk everything to hold on to Aaron's love.

Read more at www.jpbarnabyauthor.com.

About the Author

Let's get real. Yes, JP Barnaby is an award-winning romance author whose Survivor Series was heralded as one of USA Today's favorites. But what you should really know is that JP is a mental health advocate. She writes about all kinds people with mental health issues because the conversation needs to be had—out loud. Depressed people fall in love. Anxious people fall in love. Schizophrenics fall in love.

Everyone deserves to fall in love.

On a side note, JP fell in love with a super chill guy who loves her, not despite all her rips and creases but because of them. So does her 70-lb Staffy, only she does it with more fur.

Read more at www.jpbarnabyauthor.com.